The Barchester Murders

G.M. BEST

buried
river
press

ISBN 978-1-910208-08-3

Buried River Press
Clerkenwell House
Clerkenwell Green
London EC1R 0HT

www.halebooks.com

Buried River Press is an imprint of Robert Hale Ltd

2 4 6 8 10 9 7 5 3 1

Typeset in Palatino
Printed in Great Britain by Clays Limited, St Ives plc

Contents

Contents

PROLOGUE

AN OLD MAN DIES

THOMAS RIDER KNEW there was something of great significance that he had to say to someone but he could not for the life of him remember what it was. All he could recall was that it was something to do with someone's mother and that the information was both unpleasant and dangerous. There had been a time when his growing forgetfulness had annoyed him but he had long since come to accept a man entering his eighties had to expect a degree of memory loss, especially when it came to remembering recent events. He took comfort in the knowledge that what he had to say would eventually come back to him and he began thinking of happier days. Experience had taught him that it sometimes helped if he deliberately blocked out the present with its daily reminders of a growing frailty and instead took solace in recalling his childhood and youth, a time as yet unaffected by any memory loss.

His mind travelled back to when he was very young and those occasional times when his mother

7

would allow him to stay up late. He smiled as he recalled how he would sit quietly on the chair that his father had made for him and watch her preparations for bed with fascination. After she had untied her hair and permitted her long brown tresses to cascade down to her waist, she would take a brush and proceed to comb them with gentle sweeping strokes, pausing occasionally to pull out an unwanted grey hair. It had been one of his mother's few vanities because the adversities of life had by then taken away the bloom of her cheeks and begun scoring her face with a myriad of fine lines. Many years later he had read somewhere that it took 2,000 frowns to make a wrinkle and he had known at once that the information was false. His mother had never been one to frown and times of hardship had never prevented her filling their house with happiness.

He had never doubted her love for him. As if it was yesterday he relived those precious moments when he would run to embrace her, pressing his curly head against her breasts so that he could listen to the reassuring beat of her heart and smell the sweetness of her soft body. She would let him rest there for a time and then gently prize his tiny fingers from the buttons on her dress. Often, if time permitted, she would laughingly tell him a story, igniting his imagination with effortless ease. Only when his father demanded that she stop making a fool of him did she insist on him climbing off her knee. And even then she would not let him depart without a kiss.

His father had been incapable of showing that kind of love. He had been uncomfortably remote and distant all through Thomas's growing up. He could scarce recall ever seeing his father smile. What had made matters worse was his expectation that any child should be stationary and silent in his presence. Thomas had been compelled to cease playing when his father came home from work. He could still visualize him sitting in his chair and gazing into the hearth, lost in his thoughts and saying scarce a word to anyone. His father had refused to let him stay long enough at school for a good education because he had not wanted him to become cleverer than him. That was why Thomas had ended up plying the same trade as his father – making fancy knives for sale to those who visited Barchester. His mother had not approved. She had thought her son possessed the potential to make far more of his life. But, looking back on his life, Thomas had few complaints. He had always earned enough to live comfortably.

It was only once he had started working alongside his father that he had come to see his qualities. It was not just that he was a most conscientious worker and scrupulously fair in his dealings with people. Unlike some of the other knife-makers, he never wasted his hard-won earnings on gambling or drinking, but instead made his priority paying his rent and providing regular food on the table for his family. His father had sought no thanks for that because, emotionless though he appeared, he loved them. Only on one occasion had Thomas seen his father shed tears and that was on the day when his mother had died. By then her body was bent and twisted with rheumatism but his father had grieved for her loss as if she were still the beautiful young girl he had married over forty years before. The image of his father's grief-stricken face, yellow in the candlelight, was not something Thomas would ever forget. The eyes were those of a man already dead. He had not long survived her loss.

Thomas reluctantly dragged himself back into the present. His father would have told him to get a grip of himself and focus on what he needed to remember. Someone was in danger, even in the sanctuary that had become his retirement home. Yet how could evil cross the threshold of such a wonderful place as Hiram's Hospital? From the bench where he was sitting he looked out across the dappled water that sparkled in the morning sun. The sky was a wonderful blue and the birds were all silent in the heat. On the opposite shore of the gently flowing river the green grass lay like an emerald blanket covering the undulating countryside. Only a few flower-filled hedgerows and the occasional tree stood out against the surrounding hills. Surely no danger could lurk within a haven so blessed by God?

He forgot again about what he was trying to recall and a wistful smile crossed his face. Now he was too old to contemplate reaching those fields, yet as a boy he had roamed them freely. He had spent many an hour dipping for newts in murky ponds or hunting after rabbits and hares with a bow and arrow that he had fashioned himself. Pleasure had abounded in simple actions like climbing trees and collecting birds' eggs or even just beheading cow parsley with a stick. He recalled how as a child he had gazed in wonder at the ice-covered webs of spiders and the strange patterns that adorned windows and water pails in the winter months. Now he feared snow and ice lest he slip and break a bone. Then he had sledged recklessly down the white hillsides and skated across the frozen river without a care that he might slip through the ice into the water beneath. He smiled again as he revisited in his mind's eye the occasion when he and his friends had built a veritable army of snowmen with hands made blue by the cold. The icy warriors had remained standing like winter scarecrows long after the snow on the ground had melted away. Then there had been the snowball fights! Battles fought with as much courage and daring as children could muster and adults would permit.

The sound of a solitary bird broke the silence and his reverie. Suddenly it seemed bizarre to be thinking of winter on such a beautiful summer's morning. He had always preferred the summer. As a boy it had been his custom to go swimming on sunny days until that terrible day when his friend Joshua Bell had died. Weeks of heavy rain had caused the river to flow far faster than was its normal course and Joshua had been swept away and drowned. The poor lad's father was the village schoolmaster, a kind man, a Methodist who had inscribed some words from John Wesley as a text above his desk: 'Never forget an ounce of love is worth a pound of knowledge.' He could still see in his mind's eye the poor man's fingers standing out white-knuckled against the black slime that covered his dead child. He had wailed like an animal caught in a poacher's trap and it had taken all the persuasion of the minister to make poor Mr Bell hand over the body to the undertaker. His heart had shrivelled up like a plucked flower laid out in the harsh glare of the sun. All Joshua's classmates had been taken to see the corpse. Perfume had been used to mask the smell of death but they had all been terrified at seeing their friend's freckled face. It was covered with a waxy sheen like that of a dead fish.

Thomas looked out again at the river as it flowed past him. It was hard to believe that something so inviting could be so dangerous. But then danger was often something that lurked unseen until it was too late. Thomas winced. It suddenly came to him again that a friend was in danger and he had to warn him. But who? And why? It had something to do with a woman. Or was that just his imagining? As far as he could recall, he had shown little interest in women after the death of his wife all those years ago. She had meant more to him than even his mother. For days after his loss he could think of nothing but the love they had shared. Lying in his narrow bed alone, he had found himself recalling the rhythm of their lovemaking. His mouth pressed firm against hers, the intimate touch of skin to skin, the sensation that seemed to travel through his entire body and then transmit itself into her. And afterwards, he had enjoyed looking at her white nakedness, confident that each time they made love the pleasure would increase as their knowledge of each other's bodies grew. Yet it was their love that had destroyed her because she had died in childbirth. So too had the child.

That was it! He had to speak about a woman's child – a pretty but potentially evil child born of a beautiful but monstrous mother who had murdered her husband. Suddenly it all came back to him. The child's history had been hidden but now the secret was out and he had to warn the warden. How could he have been so stupid as to forget! He did not want to speak out about what he knew but he had to do so, even though it would cause much pain. He should have spoken up before. Already it might be too late! The agitated old man began to rise from the bench with the help of the walking stick that was now his constant companion on any walk he undertook. As he struggled to his feet, a shadow passed over him and he looked up to see a familiar figure standing before him.

'Oh, it's you,' he mumbled. 'I didn't hear you come to me. I'm afraid I'm a bit stiff from sitting here too long. Will you give me a hand to get up?'

A strong arm pushed him firmly back down on to the bench and Thomas felt a sharp pain in his chest. A strange coldness seemed to flow through his veins and in the few moments before he died he knew it was too late. He would never be able to warn his friend of the danger that threatened to destroy the happiness of all at Hiram's. He was no doctor but he sensed the knife had been most skilfully used and that his lifeblood was oozing from a wound near to his heart. There was no rapid flow as there might have been had he been a younger man. Thomas's chin slumped forward on to his chest. It looked as if he had simply fallen asleep. The murderer quickly moved away from the bench and headed towards the almshouse where Thomas Rider had his home. No one had seen the stabbing and to the casual observer no crime had been committed because the old man lay as if fast asleep on the garden bench.

1

HIRAM'S HOSPITAL

A WELL-DRESSED MAN, not quite six feet in height and broad shouldered, stood alone on the pretty one-arched bridge that spanned the gently flowing river. He was dressed in a grey calf-length frock coat and around his neck was a dark cravat knotted into a wide pointy bow. The fact that he had ridden earlier that day was evidenced not just by the fact he was wearing riding breeches and boots, but by the flecks of dirt that were spattered across them. Nevertheless, Anthony Trollope had spent most of the morning on foot. Busy though he was, he had been determined to take some time off his duties in order to soak up the beauty of Barchester's ancient buildings. He had especially admired the magnificent cathedral with its towering spire. In his opinion, few churches showed such grace and harmony in their external design and he now understood why the artist John Constable had painted this medieval masterpiece so frequently. It was unfortunate that the cathedral's interior was not as impressive. To his eyes the nave was too narrow and the scarcity of stained glass made it feel cold and bare. More to his taste had been the exquisite Lady's Chapel and the cathedral's beautiful cloisters.

From his vantage point on the bridge, Trollope looked across at a building that stood quite close to the water's edge. It was nothing remotely on the scale of the cathedral but it had its own picturesque beauty. His shortsighted vision somewhat blurred the scene before him but he rightly judged it was an ancient almshouse. Beyond it was an altogether grander house and at its rear what appeared to be a partly enclosed garden with a well-mown lawn. A large gravel walk ran down from this to the bridge on which he stood. Looking down over the parapet he could see a bench to his right. On it was a man dressed entirely in black; judging from his posture, he was fast asleep in the sun. Trollope sighed, wishing that he had better eyesight and the artistic skills necessary to capture such an attractive scene on canvas.

His attention was suddenly caught by the sound of music floating through the air. It was a plaintive air and prettily played on a violincello. He looked for its source and saw that three men had entered the garden of the house. His poor eyesight prevented him making out the features of any of them but he could see that one of them had taken up a seat in the summerhouse in order to play to the others. Even as he watched, one of the listeners began making his way down the gravel path towards the bench on which the sleeping man rested. His progress was slow and, as he drew nearer, Trollope could see he was old although still quite upright and burly. He was wearing a black gown and breeches and these gave him an air of authority. Once he got to his destination he reached out to awaken the sleeper by shaking his right shoulder. At once the peaceful scene took an unexpected turn because the body of the man on the bench immediately slid forwards and collapsed onto the stone-covered ground.

Without a moment's hesitation Trollope left the bridge to offer his assistance. For so large a man he moved both easily and rapidly. He ran around to the ponderous gateway that provided entrance to the almshouse and rushed into the garden, shouting that a man had collapsed by the bench near the bridge. His voice was bass and resonant and carried well. The man with the violincello immediately stopped playing. He was a small man with rather grizzled hair. Trollope rightly surmised that this must be the cleric in charge of the almshouse because he was dressed in a black frock coat, black knee breeches and black gaiters, even though, somewhat unusually for a clergyman, he sported a black handkerchief round his neck rather than a clerical collar. He was probably verging on sixty but he bore few signs of age and his eyes in particular were clear and bright behind his double glasses. The cleric immediately turned to his companion and said, 'It's fortunate that you're here, John. Your skills may be required.'

The person who had been listening to his playing was tall, athletic and strikingly handsome. Trollope thought he was probably in his mid twenties. His black curly hair set off his pale skin and his large brown eyes seemed to shine with a natural intelligence. The young man began running down the gravel path towards the bench by the bridge. Trollope ran after him and the cleric followed suit but was unable to maintain their pace. The man who had fallen was lying absolutely motionless face down on the ground. He was wearing the coarse black gown, black breeches and black buckled shoes worn by all the almshouse's inmates. His fellow resident had also not moved and appeared to be rooted to the spot with shock.

The young man knelt down and muttered, 'It's Thomas Rider,' just as the cleric arrived at the scene. 'Why don't you see to poor Benjamin Bunce. He's obviously very upset. Take him back to his room while I examine Thomas and, if possible, carry him inside with the help of this gentleman.'

'What Mr Bold says makes sense to me, providing, sir, you're willing to help us,' replied the cleric, trying to retain his composure. Then he added in explanation, 'Mr Bold is a fully qualified surgeon and I can assure you that no patient could be in better hands than his.'

Trollope willingly assented and the cleric gently but firmly then said to the standing old man, 'Come along, Bunce. Thomas is in good hands now. Mr Bold and this kind gentleman will take care of him.' Bunce nodded and some of the colour began to slowly flow back into his pale cheeks.

As the two men moved away, the young doctor signalled to Trollope not to touch the body, whispering, 'I fear Thomas Rider's beyond my care. I've already ascertained that there's no pulse and that he's not breathing.' Bold waited until he could see that the two were well on their way back to the almshouse before concluding, 'I saw no point in saying that Thomas was already dead in front of his friend. It's better that Bunce should hear the news of Rider's death when he's recovered from his initial shock.'

'It was kind of you to be so thoughtful. I'm not sure I would've had your presence of mind.'

The doctor acknowledged this praise with a smile. 'The men who live here are all very old and I'm afraid death can strike any one of them at any moment.' He looked down on the corpse sadly. 'But that doesn't lessen the pain of parting. Thomas Rider will be much missed by his friends here. He was a very kind and intelligent man.' He gave a sigh and then resumed his professional manner. 'I would be grateful if you could help me turn his body over so I can properly ascertain the cause of death. I'll have to write a report for Mr Harding to give to the authorities.'

'Mr Harding?'

'My dear sir, I am sorry. We've been remiss in not introducing ourselves properly. I'm John Bold and I've newly set up as a surgeon here in Barchester. The clerical gentleman you met is the Reverend Septimus Harding. He's the warden of Hiram's Hospital, as the almshouse here is called. He's also the precentor at Barchester Cathedral. Who are you?'

'My name is Anthony Trollope and I work as a surveyor for the Post Office. I only arrived in Barchester this morning. I left my horses at an inn under the care of my groom, who travels with me, and spent the earlier part of this morning walking around the city and viewing the cathedral. I was on the bridge admiring the almshouse when I saw this man collapse.'

'We're grateful for your assistance.'

The two men began to turn over the corpse and only then realized the cause of the old man's death. There was a deep wound in the centre of his chest. Trollope held up his hands with horror. Like the stones on which the body had lain, they were smeared red with the dead man's blood. 'My God!' he gasped. 'He's been stabbed to death!'

'And from a blow wielded with some expertise,' Bold said tersely. 'Whoever struck him did so very close to his heart.'

'You must believe me when I say that I never saw anyone stab him,' stammered Trollope. 'I genuinely thought he was simply a man asleep on a bench. The man you called Bunce thought so too. He shook him to wake him and that was when the body fell to the ground.'

'I can see from the spectacles you're wearing that you are shortsighted. Are you sure that you did not see anyone else? I can tell that poor Thomas hasn't been dead long.'

'My sight's not good but I can assure you there was no one else here. The murder must have taken place just before I arrived on the bridge.'

'That may be the case but I'm afraid I must ask you to stay here until we've reported this matter to the police.'

'Of course. And I'm very happy to help you carry the poor man to his room before the proper authorities are notified.'

'Thank you, Mr Trollope, but the police may want to see the body in situ.' He moved part of the dead man's black gown so that it covered Rider's sightless eyes. 'Our first step now must be to notify the warden and ensure that none of the residents venture down here. Mr Harding will be distraught. He looks on all the old men here as his friends.'

As the two men neared the almshouse, the cleric emerged from its main door to greet them, having encouraged Bunce to take a rest in his room. 'My apologies for not introducing myself, sir,' he said, turning towards Trollope. 'My name is Reverend Septimus Harding and I'm the warden of Hiram's Hospital. Thomas Rider is one of the twelve men under my care.'

Trollope introduced himself and Bold then conveyed the terrible news that Thomas Rider had been murdered. The warden's eyes rounded with amazement and suddenly all his authority seemed to desert him. The doctor took one look at his friend's grief-stricken face and took charge of the situation. 'Listen carefully to me, Mr Harding. I have to return to guard the corpse so you must tell Mrs Winthrop what has happened. Instruct her first to direct Mr Trollope to where he can wash the blood from his hands and then get her to fetch Inspector Blake. I'll use the time before he arrives to ascertain more fully the nature of the blow that killed poor Thomas.' The doctor turned to Trollope and explained, 'Mrs Winthrop is Mr Harding's housekeeper and a very capable woman. Not the sort to panic over what has happened even though she will be painfully shocked by the news.'

Mr Harding thanked Bold for offering such practical advice and immediately escorted Trollope into his home. It was obvious that no expense had been spared on its construction. It was a far grander building than the almshouse and had the most beautiful oriel windows. The warden led the way into his book-lined study. As far as Trollope could see there were volumes of all sorts on its shelves – not just theological works and serried ranks of collected sermons but histories, geographies, scientific works and even books of verse and fiction. Mr Harding invited him to sit down and pulled the cord to summon his housekeeper. Within a few moments she arrived.

Mrs Winthrop had the air of authority that is so often the hallmark of a woman in her position. She heard the news of the murder with a remarkable outward calmness. Only the whiteness of the knuckles on her clenched hands showed her inner turmoil at what had happened. Trollope could see that she had probably been very attractive when she was younger. She had large brown eyes and well-proportioned features. However, the years had not treated her well. Her brown hair was streaked with grey, her face was quite heavily lined, and, worst of all, her left cheek was disfigured by an ugly scar. It almost looked as if someone had slashed her with a knife. The plain clothes that she wore made it obvious that she took no interest in her figure, although she was still slim and shapely.

'I'm sure that the police will soon capture the person responsible, sir,' she blurted out in a voice that trembled only slightly. 'Though I can't think who would want to do such a terrible thing to a kindly old man.'

With admirable efficiency she immediately led Trollope out of the study to where he could wash his hands. 'Has Mr Harding been here long?' he asked curiously en route.

'He's only been warden here for ten months, sir.'

'And what about the murdered man?'

'Thomas Rider was here long before Mr Harding.' Suddenly her face lost its mask-like quality and she bit her lip in an effort to hide her emotion. 'If you don't mind, I'd prefer not to speak too much about him at present, sir. He was such a harmless man and I can't bear to think of him having been murdered.'

Outwardly Trollope had a loud, booming manner reminiscent of the kind of man who went out hunting with hounds, but that belied his true nature. He was at heart sensitive and generous-hearted. He saw at once that it would be unkind to ask the housekeeper anything more about any of the individuals caught up in the tragedy. Instead he changed the conversation to safer territory as they entered the kitchen and she provided him with a bowl of water and some soap. 'Perhaps you could tell me something about the history of this place to take both our minds off what has happened?'

'Certainly, sir, though you must appreciate that I'm no historian.'

He smiled reassuringly at her as he began to wash his hands. 'But doubtless you can tell me who was responsible for building the almshouse?'

'The hospital was founded by a wool stapler from Barchester called John Hiram. In his will he bequeathed his house and certain meadows and closes near the city to set up a charity for the support of twelve superannuated wool carders.'

'And does Hiram's Hospital still offer a home to

retired wool carders?'

She handed him a towel. 'No, sir, the wool industry has long disappeared. Now the hospital offers a place to twelve men drawn from a range of occupations. The one qualification they share in common is that the bedesmen (as they are known) must have been bred and brought up in or very near to Barchester. Each receives not only his accommodation but also one shilling and sixpence a day.' Not without a shudder, she covered the bowl of bloodied water. 'You'll forgive me, sir, but I must now go and fetch Inspector Blake. Can you make your own way back to Mr Harding's study?'

'That'll be no problem, Mrs Winthrop. Thank you for your assistance.'

When Trollope returned to the study he found Mr Harding had not moved. He was still sitting in the same chair with the same dejected posture. It was obvious from the expression on his face that he was not coping well with the situation. Trollope sat down opposite him and tried to take his mind off what had happened by engaging in small talk. 'I gather you've been warden here for less than a year, Mr Harding?' he asked. When there was no response, he added, 'Am I right?'

The warden's innate sense of courtesy overcame his silence. 'Yes, you're correct, Mr Trollope, but I've been in Barchester for over twenty years. I started my clerical career in London and then I came here after my wife died. That was back in 1830.'

'I'm sorry to hear of your loss. It must've been quite a big decision to move here.'

'Not really. I didn't feel that London was a good

place to bring up two motherless daughters and becoming a minor canon in Barchester was a very happy change from the kind of work I'd been doing. I loved in particular the music at the cathedral and willingly took on the duties of precentor when the holder of that office became ill. I can honestly say that I've never for one moment regretted being here until today.' The pain in his voice was almost tangible and his eyes spilled over with tears.

'And do your two daughters still live here?' enquired Trollope as gently as he could, determined to encourage a happier train of thought.

'Eleanor does but my other daughter, Susan, is married to the Rev. Dr Theophilus Grantly, the arch-deacon of Barchester. He's the son of the bishop. They live in the rectory at Plumstead Episcopi with the five children from his first marriage – three boys named Charles, Henry and Samuel, and two girls, Florinda and Grizzel. It was shortly after their marriage that the bishop encouraged the precentor to formally retire and I was formally appointed in his stead. Soon after-wards he also appointed me in charge of Hiram's. The role's not an onerous one. I simply have responsibility for the twelve men who are able to reside here through the generosity of the founder of this place.'

Trollope could not help but smile to himself. He suspected that Mr Harding would probably have remained a minor canon but for his daughter's choice of husband. What more might have been said between them was lost because of the sudden entry of John Bold. Both men rose rapidly to their feet. The doctor looked in the direction of the warden and wasted no time on pleasantries. 'Inspector Blake's already arrived,' he stated. 'He happened to be passing the entrance to Hiram's just as Mrs Winthrop was going out to get him. He's instructed that I move the body into the almshouse but only after he's seen you in Thomas Rider's room. He's searching Rider's possessions to see if he can find any clues as to why he's been murdered.'

'Then I'll go at once,' replied Mr Harding, looking like a rabbit caught in the glare of a poacher's lamp. 'John, will you look after Mr Trollope until I return?'

Bold nodded his assent and Mr Harding immediately left the study. Only then did Trollope ask the young doctor what his examination of the corpse had shown.

'There are no signs of any bruises arising from any struggle. It's my opinion that Thomas did not expect the blow and that the killer knew exactly where to strike. The blade was plunged almost directly into his heart. The only consolation is that I doubt whether the poor old man felt much pain. Death would've been almost instantaneous. What really puzzles me is what was the motive? I just can't see any reason why anyone would wish to kill him!'

'Are you so sure? In small communities like this it's not unknown for a tiny grievance to rankle and for passions to get out of control.'

'I hear what you say but Thomas was not the sort of person who attracts enemies. He was honest in his word and kind to anyone in need.'

'And presumably that's why Mr Harding is so upset?'

'In part but I'm pretty sure that he will be holding

himself personally responsible for what has happened because Mr Rider was under his protection. He takes the welfare of the men here very seriously.'

'Have you known him long?'

'Since I was a boy. My father was a successful surgeon in London but much of his wealth was invested in property here. As a family we often used to visit Barchester. At first my sister Mary and I were very lonely but Mr Harding and his daughters then befriended us. I still regard him as my greatest friend. When you interrupted us in the garden I was listening to him play his violincello. It gives Mr Harding great pleasure and it's an easy way for me to show my gratitude for his kindness over the years.' The sincere way in which this was said conveyed Bold's deep affection for him.

'So what brings you to Barchester now?'

'I live here. While I was still training to become a physician, my father decided to retire here in the company of my sister. They took up residence in a villa not far from Hiram's and I stayed with them every holiday. When my father died just over twelve months ago, I decided not to sell his house. I'd just completed my qualifications and it seemed an ideal opportunity to begin my work in a place that I knew.' He gave Trollope a rueful smile. 'Unfortunately the nine doctors already in residence haven't greeted my arrival with pleasure and so far I've had little opportunity to use my medical gifts except among the poor who can't pay.'

Trollope looked at the handsome doctor and wondered whether his decision to stay in Barchester owed something to the warden's other daughter. 'Mr Harding tells me that he lives here with his daughter Eleanor, but I've seen no sight of her,' he said, to see how Bold would react. The immediate blush that came to the doctor's cheeks confirmed that his conjecture was accurate.

'Eleanor was here earlier this morning but she went out in the small carriage that Mr Harding has newly purchased for her. Her sister and brother-in-law accompanied her.'

'Pardon me for saying so, Mr Bold, but I'm surprised that the post of warden should carry with it enough income for a carriage to be kept.'

Bold looked slightly discomforted. 'I'll be honest with you, sir. None here have anything but good to say of Mr Harding, but many in Barchester aren't happy with the arrangements at Hiram's Hospital. The money paid out to the bedesmen is but a tiny element of the income that's derived from John Hiram's estate. The land that in his day was used for farming is now covered with rows of houses and the value of the property has therefore increased beyond all measure. It's a scandal that so wealthy a foundation contributes so little to the poor of the city.'

'So does the bulk of the income therefore go to the warden?'

'A sizeable proportion does. I believe Mr Harding gets about eight hundred pounds per year, which is probably about four times what the post deserves. I suspect just as much money ends up in the hands of Mr Chadwick, who acts as the steward for Hiram's property.'

'From what you say the post of warden is a very snug sinecure,' Trollope replied drily. 'If Mr Harding is the good man you describe, why's he not uncomfortable about that?'

'When a man's appointed to a post it's natural that he should accept the income allotted without much enquiry. I think it says much for Mr Harding's character that one of his first actions as warden was to increase the payment made to the bedesmen.'

'And was that well received?'

Bold shook his head. 'On the contrary. It encouraged some of the old men to think they should be getting even more and it offended the other members of the cathedral clergy, especially Mr Harding's son-in-law, Dr Grantly. '

'Why?' asked Trollope, genuinely puzzled.

'He told Mr Harding that he was setting a very bad precedent in reducing his own income, even if it was by only a small amount. He said that the bedesmen had no need of extra money because all their wants are supplied. They have warm houses, good clothes and a plentiful diet.' Bold paused and smiled. 'I should also add that Dr Grantly simply will not hear anyone criticize what the Church does. I think he'd consign all those who question what Hiram's money is being spent on to darkness and perdition if he could!'

'You make him sound a monster.'

'No, in his own way he's a good man, but Dr Grantly tends to confuse the Church with Christianity. That's why he's currently encouraging Mr Harding to think that he can justify his income by spending much of it on the cathedral choir and on the publication of collections of ancient church music.'

'But you think otherwise about the matter?'

Bold hesitated several moments before replying. 'Yes, I do. I love and respect Mr Harding but I think it's wrong that he receives so much. I see many diseases that could easily be prevented if the money from Hiram's bequest were put to better purpose.'

'And have you told Mr Harding that?'

'Not in so many words. He's such a kind man that I fear to cause him pain on the matter.'

Trollope suspected that Bold's reticence probably stemmed from his attachment to Eleanor Harding, but he chose not to say so. An uncomfortable silence filled the room and it was broken only by the return of Mr Harding. A very tall and unprepossessing man dressed in a blue frock coat and white trousers accompanied him. He had dark and rather lank hair, heavy lidded and bulbous brown eyes, a bony narrow nose that was slightly misshapen, a wide mouth that was thin-lipped, and hollow cheeks that were heavily scarred by smallpox. 'Permit me to introduce you, Mr Trollope, to Inspector Blake,' said the warden in a voice that betrayed his inner tension.

There was no indication of any warmth in the policeman's handshake. 'A terrible crime has been committed here, Mr Trollope. A terrible crime,' he stated solemnly in a gruff voice. He paused as if to give time for this information to sink into the minds of all three men and then added, 'I've seen poor Mr Rider's body.' He raised an eyebrow and pursed his lips as if somehow this would convey to all of them the horror of what he had been forced to face. 'And

I've asked Mr Bold to provide me with a full medical report. I've not yet met a criminal who can hide from good evidence!' He stared hard at Trollope. 'You may be a stranger here, but make no mistake, sir, I'll find the murderer and ensure that the cord goes round his neck!'

'I think that I would prefer to be described as a visitor to Barchester rather than a stranger,' observed Trollope.

'A visitor is a stranger until more is known of his background. And we know nothing of yours, sir. Would you mind telling me how you come to be here?'

'I've no objection but I can assure you that it won't help you with your enquiries.'

'I'll be the judge of that,' snapped back the inspector rather pompously.

It was immediately obvious to Trollope that he was being viewed as the prime suspect. Just a short time earlier he had been standing on a bridge enjoying the morning sunshine. Now the day looked as if it might end with him being confined to a prison cell as a suspected murderer!

2

THE INVESTIGATION BEGINS

TROLLOPE TRIED NOT to show his alarm and stated as calmly as he could, 'Sir, my name is Anthony Trollope as I've told these gentlemen. I'm here because I work for the Post Office as a surveyor and at present I'm travelling across the south-west of England.'

Inspector Blake gazed back at him. Distrust was writ large on his face. 'May I ask for what purpose?' he replied in a tone that implied it was only a matter of time before Trollope confessed to the crime.

'You'll be aware that in recent years the Post Office has created a national network for delivering letters as a consequence of Mr Rowland Hill creating the Penny Black. Ten years ago I was sent to work out the best routes for the post to take in Ireland. I did such a good job that I am now sent to improve the service in this region.'

'And so what exactly does that entail, Mr Trollope?' questioned the inspector, only marginally pacified by the explanation he had been given. 'Please elaborate.'

Trollope tried not to show his annoyance. 'The first

thing that I have to do is check that those who work for the Post Office are not cheating the company by charging for long routes that are unnecessary. In that process I talk to local people and ascertain what they think should be happening. I then try to find new and better routes for postmen, ensuring that none require them to travel more than sixteen miles per day on foot. To achieve that I travel widely, exploring every lane and every possible shortcut across open fields. I also make sure that whatever routes I devise tie in with the mail being transported by night mail-carts and with the up-mail from London.'

'It sounds an onerous task,' Mr Harding commented, clearly showing the inspector that he had confidence in the truth of his visitor's story.

'It is. I usually rise as soon as it is light and travel about forty miles each day on horseback. My only companion is the groom who sees to my horses. I've two hunters of my own and can hire a third if necessary. However, you need not feel sorry for me. I love the work. It's far better than being tied to an office and I get to meet all kinds of people from all walks of life.'

'So where do you live?' interrupted Blake brusquely.

'My home is still in Ireland.'

A look of disdain crossed the inspector's face. 'Can you supply me with your address?'

Trollope hid his irritation with difficulty and retorted acidly, 'Yes, I can, sir, providing that does not mean the authorities will needlessly worry my wife. I don't want her to know I'm involved in a murder enquiry. It would only serve to needlessly alarm her.'

'I can assure you that we won't bother her, sir,

unless circumstances change.'

'You mean, Inspector, unless you think I'm the murderer of Thomas Rider!' exclaimed Trollope angrily. 'Damn it, man, I'll swear on the Bible that I'm entirely innocent in this matter.'

'That won't be necessary, Mr Trollope,' interjected Mr Harding, who had clearly become increasingly uncomfortable at the way Blake was interrogating his guest. 'I believe you.'

The inspector sniffed. 'The trouble is, Mr Harding, that you believe the best in everyone. I've learned to be more circumspect before I accept a man's word. There's a lot of evil in the world and I'm afraid deceit comes natural to some men.'

'The world is also full of men who are naturally honest and good.'

'Bah! Tell that to poor Thomas Rider,' responded the inspector contemptuously.

This cruel taunt totally silenced the warden but served to further incense Trollope. 'It's ridiculous for you to view me with suspicion, sir! Have you no common sense? If I was the person responsible for killing the old man why did I then come running to give the alarm? Surely I would simply have run off so none could link me with the crime? The plain truth of the matter is that when I entered the hospital's grounds I assumed that Mr Rider had simply been taken ill. I was completely taken aback when I discovered that he'd been stabbed.'

'That's as may be, sir, but I would still like to corroborate your story by speaking to your groom and I'd be grateful if you would give me the details of your supervisor at the Post Office so that I can also check that you are in Barchester on the company's business.'

'Is that really necessary?' intervened Bold. 'This man is being poorly paid for his kindness. He simply alerted us to what he'd seen.'

Trollope saw the inspector was not going to change his attitude and interposed to bring the matter to a close. 'Do not fret, Mr Bold. Neither you nor I may like the inspector's manner, but I suppose he's merely doing his duty. People would think less of him if he did not seek to verify my story. Give me a sheet of paper and I'll write down all the information that he requires.'

Trollope sat at Mr Harding's desk to write what was wanted. Blake took the sheet and glanced at its contents without the hint of any gratitude. 'Thank you, sir,' he said curtly. 'Until I receive assurances that you are who you say you are, I must ask that you don't leave Barchester.'

'I understand and I give you my word I'll stay in the city.'

'In which inn have you taken up residence?'

'None as yet. This morning on my arrival I simply left my luggage at The Sun, the inn where my groom is tending to my two horses. It was not my intention to stay in Barchester overnight.'

'It's fine for their needs but I wouldn't advise you to stay there,' observed Bold. 'The beds are very uncomfortable and the food is poor.'

'Then where would you recommend?'

'If you wish, you may stay here,' offered Mr Harding. 'I've a spare room you can use.'

Trollope was moved by the warden's kindness but shook his head. 'That's a very generous offer but I can't possibly accept it.'

'Why not?'

'You have enough to do without coping with me.'

Mr Harding shook his head. 'Nonsense. I'd welcome your presence, especially as I've a daughter and I've no way of knowing whether the murderer is still around. I'm sure both she and I will feel safer with you also in the house.'

Trollope considered this unexpected response and recognized there was sense in what the warden said. His presence might well make it less likely that the killer would risk striking again. He smiled and warmly shook Mr Harding's hand. 'Very well, I accept. I'd much rather stay with you than reside in an inn.' He turned and looked at the inspector and added, 'That is, of course, providing you're comfortable with such an arrangement?'

'It's not what I would do if I were in Mr Harding's position, but if that's what is agreed, so be it. I'll arrange for a message to be delivered to your groom so that your baggage may be sent here from the inn after I've questioned him. What's the man's name?'

'John Turner. Tell him the horses will have to remain at The Sun until I'm free to leave here. He must get appropriate accommodation for himself there.'

For the next few moments the inspector turned his attention to elucidating more information about the dead man and, once that was done, he offered to make arrangements for the body of Mr Rider to be collected and taken away.

'You'll forgive me, sir, if I decline your offer,' Mr Harding replied. 'This place was Thomas's home and I don't want him taken from it until he's laid in the earth. The other bedesmen will want to pay their last respects to him and they're all too frail to travel far.'

'As you wish, Mr Harding,' acceded the inspector. 'But I must ask that you let me question all of them. One or more of them may be able to shed light on Thomas Rider's murder.'

'None of them have yet been told what's happened,' interpolated Bold. 'Something needs to be said to them first. They're not so old that they can't see we are caught up in some terrible tragedy. They're aware that Rider has collapsed and some of them saw Mrs Winthrop bring in Mr Blake.'

Mr Harding flinched. The prospect of informing the bedesmen made him feel very uncomfortable. 'You're right to remind me that I've not fulfilled my duty. I must speak with all my friends and seek to comfort them before any questioning can commence. John, I know that you've medical duties elsewhere and therefore can't stay here much longer. However, I'd be grateful if you would tell Bunce what has happened before you leave and before I release the news to the others. While he is doing that, I suggest, Mr Blake, that you ring the gatehouse bell three times. That will signal I'm to hold a meeting in the quad for everyone. Mr Trollope, I'd be grateful if you would find Mrs Winthrop and then help her to assemble the feebler bedesmen. While you are doing all of that I'll try and compose my mind so I can think what I should say to them.'

All three men did as they were bid. Trollope discovered that the quadrangle to which the warden referred was a quiet haven from which the residents could easily view the flitting fish in the river or look across to the rich green meadows on the other side of the river. It was bordered on one side by a row of riverside seats, on the second by the almshouse, on the third by the gable end of the warden's home, and on the fourth by part of the garden's high wall and some overhanging trees. A stone-flagged path had been laid all around its perimeter and at its centre. The more physically fit bedesmen entered the quadrangle quite quickly once the inspector tolled the bell but it took a while for Trollope and Mrs Winthrop to assemble the others. As they did this the black-gowned bedesmen gathered in small groups to share their anxieties, looking like a crows' parliament. Only Bunce stood apart, his head deeply bowed.

The old men all took off their black hats when Mr Harding entered the quad. He walked over to the centre and wiped the nervous perspiration from his brow. 'My friends, I want to say a few words to you about a very upsetting event that has taken place here within Hiram's.' Not a sound could be heard from any of the men. 'You may have heard from Bunce that poor Thomas collapsed this morning.' A few nodded. 'There's no easy way to say this but I regret to inform you that he's dead.' There was a moment of stunned silence and then this was followed by a murmur of collective sadness. The ashen-faced warden continued grimly, 'And I regret even more to have to tell you that he was murdered – stabbed to death.' This announcement sent visible shock waves through them. The bedesmen were used to their number being depleted by death but never before had one of them been untimely plucked from life by the hand of another. 'That's why Inspector Blake is here,' concluded Mr Harding. 'He's determined to discover who was responsible and to bring the villain to justice.'

All eyes turned on the policeman. 'Yes, gentlemen, and I'll require your help. I therefore want to speak with each of you individually to see what you may or may not know about what's happened here this morning.'

The thought of being questioned by the police alarmed the old men and Mr Harding spent the next few minutes trying to allay their fears. Watching him at work, Trollope could see why John Bold held the warden in such high regard. He had a natural capacity to put people at their ease. Unfortunately, on this occasion even his skills were not entirely effective. Most of the bedesmen felt it was bad enough that a murderer had entered their sanctuary without then having to face an interrogation. Eventually Mr Harding judged he would have to be present when each of them was interviewed as a means of reassuring them. The inspector concurred with such an arrangement but only on condition that the warden would not interfere with his questioning of them.

'May I ask, Mr Trollope, that you continue to help Mrs Winthrop?' Mr Harding asked. 'I think she'll require some assistance to bring the weaker ones to my study and then return them to the almshouse.'

'I'm willing to help in any way I can.'

'I suggest you bring them in alphabetical order so that none can feel unfairly singled out by the order in which they're seen,' said the inspector.

The inspector and the warden went back to the house. Blake sat behind the warden's desk and indicated that Mr Harding should take a chair at ninety degrees to it. 'I'd like you to observe every one of them side on. See if you can detect any sign of guilt or unease as each answers my questions, but don't interrupt unless I indicate that you can. Before they start arriving, give me a list of their names, and before each man enters give me some information about him.'

Mr Harding took a piece of paper off his desk and wrote down all the bedesmen's names in alphabetical order. Then he passed the sheet to the inspector. 'As you can see, the first man to arrive will be Elias Bell.'

'And what should I know about him?'

'He was a respected tradesman in his day but his mind has become very confused in recent months. I doubt whether he'll be able to tell us anything.'

The warden's assessment proved an accurate one. When Elias Bell entered the room, he could not walk without the assistance of the housekeeper. Once she had sat him down, he looked across at the inspector with vacant eyes. He kept rubbing his pinched-up nose and sharp chin with fingers that trembled uncontrollably. It was obvious from his response to Blake's first questions that he had not even registered that Rider was dead. All he kept repeating was that he had no complaint to make and he hoped Thomas would recover.

'Don't worry, Inspector, I think you'll find the next bedesman much more helpful,' whispered

Mr Harding as Bell was removed from the room. 'Benjamin Bunce may be over eighty but he's still an astute man. Moreover, many of the bedesmen confide in him because he's the most senior, having been here the longest. Indeed I regard him as much as a friend as a ward.' He looked at Blake's stern face and added, 'Please be gentle. He'll try not to show it but I know he'll be grieving deeply for the loss of his friend. He and Thomas Rider were very close.'

Bunce entered the room unassisted. The vitality of his manner and the hint of ruddiness in his cheeks made it obvious that the passing of the years had not yet wreaked their full havoc on him. His deep blue eyes, though slightly watery from recently shed tears, had an almost mesmeric quality and gave him an air of natural authority. He stood with his gnarled hands resting on his staff, awaiting their permission to sit.

Once this had been granted, Blake asked, 'Are you and the others happy here, Mr Bunce?'

The old man's face visibly tightened at what he clearly took to be a slur on his home. 'We've no reason not to be,' he replied abruptly. 'We've everything we could want – a good home and plenty to eat and a very kind master in Mr Harding, who also sees to our spiritual needs.'

'Then can you shed any light on why Thomas Rider should have been brutally murdered?'

'No, I can't. He was a good man with no enemies.' For a moment Blake thought Bunce's calm façade was going to break down, but somehow the man mastered his grief. 'All I know is that something was bothering him recently.'

'Did he give you any clue about what that was?'

'I tried to get him to tell me but he declined.' Bunce turned and looked apologetically in Mr Harding's direction. 'I'm sorry, your reverence. I should've told you because I'm sure Thomas would have confided in you.'

'Don't worry yourself, Bunce. You weren't to know this terrible thing was going to happen.'

The inspector grunted to indicate that he thought Bunce should have acted differently. 'Can you think of anyone who might know more than you do?'

'Possibly Jeremiah Smith or John Gaunt. Both were very close to Thomas.'

Blake made a mark next to their names on his list. 'And is there anyone here you don't trust?'

'There's one here who should not be in my opinion. Abel Handy loves to create mischief, though I'm not saying he had a hand in Thomas's murder.'

'Now, Bunce, please remember what I told you', intervened Mr Harding. 'There's good in every man.'

'There isn't much good, I'm thinking, in what Abel Handy does, your reverence. He loves making trouble and spying and poking into things that don't concern him!'

'I know all about Mr Handy,' interrupted the inspector. 'For years that stonemason was this city's most dangerous radical. Whenever there was any trouble in Barchester you could almost guarantee he would be involved in it. For that reason I have never understood why the cathedral authorities permitted his retirement here. '

'Because the poor man lost his ability to work

whilst working on the cathedral façade. As I'm sure you're aware, Inspector, he fell from some scaffolding, shattering one leg beyond repair and breaking his thigh.'

'But the fall was almost certainly occasioned by him having drunk too much,' muttered Blake. 'That's why so many in the town offered him no pity when the accident happened. They saw his fall as a judgement sent by God.'

The inspector saw Bunce nod in agreement. He asked him a few more questions but without gleaning anything of use. 'It's obvious that you know no reason for the murder of Thomas Rider, but others among the bedesmen may. I want you to keep your eyes and ears open in case one of them lets slip some clue about the motive for the murder. Will you do that for me?'

Bunce nodded willingly and, as he left, he tried to offer some comfort to the downhearted warden. 'I'm certain God will see us all through this mess, your reverence,' he muttered.

Mr Harding acknowledged his kind words and then announced, 'The next person you will meet, Inspector, is a former wealthy cutler called Jonathan Crumple. He's a meek man and I think by temperament a humorous and kindly one, but years of ill treatment at the hands of his children have left him with a melancholy that he cannot hide.'

'I know him. He let his children waste his fortune. I begin to think that this place specializes in possessing men of poor judgement!'

'It was misguided love rather than a lack of judgement that caused the problem.'

Blake looked at the warden with disdain. 'I'm not sure I see the distinction.'

What more might have been said was lost by Crumple's arrival. Although almost seventy, he looked younger because of his bright blue eyes and apple-red cheeks. 'Are you all happy here, Mr Crumple?' asked the inspector, repeating the question he had asked Bunce.

'I can't speak for all the others but I can testify that I've known neither sorrow nor trouble since I came here.' He looked at the warden. 'It's a great blessing to have Mr Harding look after us.'

'So you know of no reason why someone here would murder Thomas Rider?'

'None. Thomas were a good man.' Crumple's lips began to quiver as he fought back tears. 'I shall miss him. He were very kind to me, especially when I first arrived here.'

A few more questions elicited nothing of use. Blake dismissed him. He put his head into his hands and pushed his fingers through his hair with frustration. 'I've no desire to grow old if it reduces me to such a pointless existence as that man has!' he exclaimed. 'How can anyone be so oblivious to what's going on around him!'

'Unfortunately age tends to make people more self-centred,' responded the warden, shrugging his shoulders. 'Their sole concern becomes what might happen to them rather than what might be happening in the life of another. You'll find that the next on your list, Billy Gazy, is far worse than poor Crumple in that respect.'

When Mrs Winthrop brought Gazy in, the only indication of life was the way the old man repeatedly rubbed his bleared eyes with the cuff of his bedesman's gown. All Gazy could say in response to any question was 'I don't know' and this was said in a tone that sounded like a bleating old sheep.

The next name on Blake's list was that of John Gaunt but Mrs Winthrop sought permission to bring in a different man. 'I thought you might not mind if I brought Job Skulpit here instead, though it's not yet his turn. I think Mr Gaunt is too upset to be questioned at this juncture. I've given Mr Trollope the task of trying to calm him down.'

Blake turned to the warden. 'Should I read anything into this delay in meeting John Gaunt?' he asked.

'No, I think not. John has least reason to fear seeing you because he spent all his working life with the police. He's a former gaoler from London's Newgate prison.'

'Then how did he come to retire here?'

'He was born in Barchester and returned here when declining health prevented him retaining his employment at the prison. Although I was not then the warden, I put in a good word for him and helped secure a place for him here. His closest friend was Thomas Rider. He'll be genuinely distraught at his death.'

'Very well, I'll see him later. Who's this Skulpit?'

'A former tailor. He's a bit weak-minded but basically a good man.'

'Show in Mr Skulpit, Mrs Winthrop.'

The housekeeper did as she was instructed.

Unfortunately, during his brief wait Skulpit's nerves had reached such a pitch that he could do little but weep when he entered the room. His face was almost completely obscured by a large handkerchief that he was using to mop up his tears. Round shouldered and partly crippled with arthritis, he kept gulping almost like a fish out of water in a vain attempt to control his emotions. It was not until Blake roared, 'For heaven's sake, pull yourself together man!', that a red-eyed face emerged from behind the handkerchief. The poor man's distress had served to emphasize all its worst features – the heavily lined forehead, the long nose, the thin cheeks and the weak mouth. Skulpit squinted painfully at the inspector because his former trade had ruined his eyesight and Blake inwardly groaned because he appreciated that the bedesman could scarce see!

The inspector soon tired of Skulpit's ignorance and he demanded Abel Handy should be brought before him instead. Handy was a well-built man and it was evident that he still had great strength in his large hands, but any hopes the inspector had of him being the possible killer were instantly dispelled when he entered the room. It was obvious the former stone-mason had not properly recovered from the appalling injuries he had sustained at the time of his fall and so there was no way that he could have retained his balance to execute the attack on Rider. Handy hobbled slowly into the study and sat down without being invited to do so, placing his crutch on one side of him and his stick on the other. There was something about the truculent and cruel look in his eyes and the furtive way that he gazed around the room that communicated the man's inherent wickedness.

'Do you know anything about what has led to Thomas Rider's murder?'

Handy stared back sullenly. 'If I do, what's it worth?' he answered in a voice that was coarse and rough.

The inspector raised his eyebrows. 'What do you mean?'

Handy smirked. 'Information's always worth summat to them who wants to know.'

'Damn it, man, it'll be worth your avoiding prison because if you're not more cooperative that's where you'll go!'

''Twas only a joke, sir.'

'This is no joking matter, and if you're not more civil you'll find yourself ejected from this almshouse!' yelled an incensed inspector.

Handy refused to be browbeaten. 'There you're wrong, sir. It's not in yer power to make me lose my place here – indeed, even the warden 'ere can't get rid of me. It's the rule that once you're in Hiram's only death can remove you – as poor Mr Rider 'as discovered to his cost!'

Blake frowned. 'Have you no sympathy for the murdered man?'

'Why should I? He were like a number of 'em in this place. Grateful without cause.' Handy looked sneeringly at Mr Harding. 'Too many of the bedesmen think they owe everything to the warden's generosity. In fact, he's robbing us of what is ourn by right.'

Blake saw Mr Harding's face flush but the warden

did not jump to his own defence. Could it be that there was some truth in Handy's allegation? The inspector suddenly felt the murder case might have more behind it than he had originally envisaged. He muttered sharply, 'Explain yourself, sir!'

'We wants what John Hiram left us. We should be getting hundreds of pounds not the pittance that we receive,' replied Handy scornfully. 'I'd petition the bishop and write to the press if I 'ad my way but most of the men 'ere were born with no pluck in 'em. They get cowed at the sight of a gentleman's waistcoat or a parson's collar.'

'I've not come to discuss the rights and wrongs of your situation here, Handy. As far as I can tell you get more than you deserve. You weren't brought here to be made a rich man and, even if you were, you'd be incapable of writing to anyone because you can't spell your name let alone pen a letter.' He looked at Handy's unrepentant visage and disliked what he saw. 'If I had my way you'd be in the poor house,' he added with a gesture that showed his distaste for the man.

Mr Harding sat ill at ease throughout this exchange because he knew there were others who felt Hiram's money was not being directed properly, even though his son-in-law had tried to make him think otherwise. He therefore made no attempt to contradict the bedesman and responded quietly, 'Abel, I think this is not the time or place to discuss this matter. Not when Thomas Rider lies dead on his bed. If you want to speak more on this matter you must seek a more opportune time. You may not like your position here, but you're an observant man and I suspect there may be more helpful things that you can tell the inspector than what you've so far said.'

Even the ungracious Handy was not immune to this argument. He nodded in a surly fashion and then replied, 'I've no idea why Mr Rider were killed but I can tell ye that the murder must've been done by someone 'ere at the hospital.'

'And why should I believe anything you say on this matter?' Blake demanded sceptically.

The goodwill generated by the earlier words of the warden was instantly dissipated by the inspector's distrust. 'I know the police. Yer'd pin the murder on me if you could! Unfortunately yer can see I'm a cripple!'

'Don't expect any sympathy from me about your condition. You fell from that scaffolding because you'd been drinking too much!'

'Aye, and I suffer for it every day.' Handy's mouth tightened and a bitter smile twisted his lips. 'But that's why I can vouch no stranger entered through the gateway of the almshouse this morning. You see, my injuries largely confine me to my room and I spend most of my time looking out of my window. It faces the entrance and I like to see who passes by and who enters or leaves. I can guarantee that no stranger entered Hiram's Hospital until that Mr Trollope ran in.' His smile took on a more sinister appearance. 'You don't have to search far for yer killer, Mr Blake. The murderer were no passing stranger. Thomas Rider were killed by someone 'ere.'

'You mean one of the bedesmen?'

'I doubt it. Most of 'em are either half dead or too weak livered.' He chuckled mischievously and his voice dropped as if to convey the significance of his next few words. 'You see, there be far more able-bodied people who could've done it.'

'Who?'

'Well, for a start there's Mr Harding and both his daughters, and, of course, the archdeacon, Dr Grantly. Nor should yer forget that young surgeon, Mr Bold. He's always 'anging around 'ere.'

'You're not seriously suggesting that any of them are involved in Rider's death!' said Blake incredulously.

The bedesman gave a malicious smile and shrugged his shoulders. 'I'm not suggesting anything, Mr Blake, other than that murderers who use a knife aren't usually old and infirm. Yer can draw yer own conclusions!'

3

THE OTHER SUSPECTS

ABEL HANDY'S INSINUATIONS upset Mr Harding so much that the inspector was compelled to curtail the interview. Blake recognized that the warden's reaction could be that of an innocent man wrongly maligned, but he equally saw that it could stem from the allegations having contained some truth. He thought it unlikely that a man of Mr Harding's reputation would commit a murder, but he was not so sure about the rest of his family or Mr Bold? The resulting tense atmosphere was not helped by the entry of the next bedesman, Gregory Moody, because he was Handy's closest associate. Moody had always taken pleasure in mocking the warden behind his back, calling him 'old Catgut' in order to deride his violincello playing. Mr Harding was aware of this and understandably feared that Moody would choose to spread yet more innuendo against him and those he loved. This generated a degree of hostility in the warden's manner that the inspector could not help but notice and be surprised at.

For years Moody had been the city's gravedigger and so he was well known to Blake. There had been a distant time when, despite his profession, he had been much in demand in Barchester because of his wit and good humour. Looking at him now, it was hard to see why. Everything about him gave the impression of meanness, especially his dirty face with its narrow eyes, sharp nose, thin lips and unshaven chin. 'May I sit down, sir?' he mumbled, wiping his mouth with the back of his right hand. 'I suffer much these days from rheumatism.'

Mr Harding knew this was a lie. Moody was physically still quite fit for his age, but he liked to pretend otherwise. He enjoyed exaggerating every ache and pain. 'No, you can stand,' he said curtly.

'That's most unlike ye, Mr Harding. Yer must be worn out by this terrible business,' the bedesman replied without a hint of sincerity in his voice. 'Perhaps some of Mr Hiram's money should've been spent on securing our safety rather than on buying cathedral music and then this 'ere murder wouldn't 'ave 'appened.'

'Don't be impertinent or I'll have you taken to the city lock-up for the night!' barked Blake angrily.

Moody seemed to sense that he had overstepped the mark and fell silent until the inspector began questioning him. However, in his responses he could hardly utter a sentence without conveying resentment at his lot. Frowning with frustration, Blake opted to draw the interview to an early close rather than persevere with such an untrustworthy witness. He wiped his brow with his handkerchief and tried hard not to show his disappointment that he had so far failed to uncover any clue as to why Rider had been killed. Blake looked at the list that the warden had given him. At least the next man due before him was one of Rider's friends and if anyone knew what had been worrying Rider, it ought to be those closest to him.

'I'm sure that you will find Jeremiah Smith more helpful,' Mr Harding commented before Mrs Winthrop showed the man in. 'He worked in the same trade as Rider and the two men were friends long before they entered here. Both men had a high reputation for not only the quality of their work but also their honest dealings with people. You can trust what he says.'

Jeremiah Smith entered the study hesitantly and Blake looked him up and down. The former cutler was short of stature and rather dumpy in appearance but there was a frailty about him that could not be hidden. The skin on his lined face was as white as starched linen and it had an almost see-through quality. A slight puffiness around his eyes bore testimony to the distress he had experienced on hearing of his friend's murder. His breathing sounded heavy and laboured. Yet Smith still carried with him an air of integrity, both in the way that he moved and in the look of his grey eyes. His white hair added to the impression that here was a venerable man.

'Mr Harding tells me that you were a good workman in your time, Mr Smith.'

'That I were, sir,' he replied hoarsely but with a touch of pride. 'None better, though I say so myself, till age caught up with me.' He stretched out his gnarled and brown-blotched hands towards the inspector. 'I lost the steady touch required.'

'But you've not lost your wits, have you?'

'No, that I 'aven't, sir.'

'So tell me what might have led to the death of your friend, Mr Rider.'

Almost at once Smith's whole demeanour changed. The honesty in his expression seemed to drain away and he looked as if he would rather be anywhere else than in the warden's study. 'I don't know, sir,' he said bleakly.

'But you must have given the matter some thought.'

The bedesman's face remained deeply troubled. 'I 'ave, sir, and I think it were the work of the devil!'

'The devil does not use a knife, Mr Smith. I can assure you a human agency is at work here. I'm told by Mr Bunce that something was bothering Thomas Rider in the days before he died. Is that right?'

Smith hesitated and then nodded. 'Yes, something had deeply upset 'im.'

'Did he tell you what that was?'

For a moment it looked as if Smith was going to try and leave the room, but then he turned and looked at Mr Harding in the way that a dog looks to its master for guidance.

Mr Harding tried to give him a reassuring smile. 'Jeremiah, if you know what was troubling Thomas you should tell the inspector.'

'I'm afraid I can't do that, sir,' muttered Smith. 'I promised Thomas that I wouldn't tell no one.'

Anger flooded over the inspector and he shouted contemptuously, 'What utter nonsense! The man's dead and so your promise means absolutely nothing. Tell us what you know at once.'

'A promise is a promise,' protested Smith.

The inspector slammed his fist on the desk. 'Mr Harding, order this idiot to tell us what he knows!'

The warden looked distinctly uncomfortable. 'I am sorry, Inspector, but you can't expect me to order a man to go against the dictates of his conscience. However, I will try to persuade him that he is being foolish.' He moved over to where the old man was sitting and put his right hand on Smith's shoulder. 'Jeremiah, I appreciate that you wish to keep your word to your friend, but think what has happened here today. Thomas was brutally murdered. We have to find out who murdered him and for all we know your information may be critical in helping us.'

Tears came into Smith's eyes but he slowly shook his head from side to side. 'I'm sorry, Mr Harding, but I promised and if you knew what it was I don't think you'd want me to speak out in front of the police.'

A further appeal from the warden might have weakened his resolve had not Blake chosen that moment to lose his temper. 'You'll tell me what you know this instant or I'll have you clapped in a cell for obstruction of justice. And if you then still refuse, I'll have the gaoler throw away the key and you can rot within its walls till you die!'

Far from helping, the tirade resulted in the bedesman refusing to answer any more questions. A stubborn look appeared in his face that augured ill for obtaining any more information from him. After exploding at him some more, Blake ordered him out of the study, saying that he would have him arrested as an accessory to the crime if he remained silent. It was left to Mr Harding to offer more conciliatory advice before Smith left them. His voice was as friendly as the inspector's had been hostile. 'Sleep on the matter, Jeremiah, and I think you'll see that it makes sense to talk with us. I suggest that you come to me in the morning if you've changed your mind and then I can arrange for you to meet with Mr Blake again.'

'Mr Harding, I think you need to run a tighter ship,' Blake said scathingly once Smith had departed. 'The men here do not recognize authority!'

The warden blushed but refused to be intimidated. 'I don't think, sir, that you can expect a man who has made a promise to his closest friend to break it without first struggling with his conscience. I'll send Bunce round to see Jeremiah later this evening and I'm confident that he'll persuade him to tell us what he knows tomorrow. Have patience.'

'It's difficult to be patient when I've sat here all afternoon and made virtually no progress on this matter,' protested Blake. He glared at Mr Harding as if he was some kind of naïve child in want of parental guidance. 'Let's quickly see the rest and get this wretched business finished. I've had more than enough for one day. My head's beginning to thump! Who's left?'

'As you can see from your list, there are just three more: Matthew Spriggs, Reuben Wilson and, of course, John Gaunt.'

The two interviews that followed were very perfunctory. Matthew Spriggs was a much younger man than the other bedesmen but hideous in his appearance because he had suffered extreme burns from falling into a fire when drunk. One eye was burnt out and one cheek burnt through and the rest of his face was badly scarred. He had sustained such injuries to the rest of his body that returning to a life of employment had been rendered impossible. One arm hung entirely useless at his side and Blake judged that his physical disability ruled him out as a suspect. Spriggs told them nothing helpful. Nor did Reuben Wilson, whose pale face looked as if it had been permanently dusted with a fine coating of flour. The former miller simply confirmed what they already knew – that Thomas Rider had been visibly upset in recent days. He claimed that he knew nothing about the cause.

A very unhappy Inspector Blake gathered together the few notes he had made during the interviews and furiously shoved them into his pocket. 'Mr Harding, I've had enough! I'm not going to wait for John Gaunt to compose himself. I shall return to the police station in order to write an initial report and set in motion the checks on whether Mr Trollope is who he says he is. If he is, then I can only hope that by the time I return tomorrow morning Jeremiah Smith has thought better of his refusal to speak with us and that John Gaunt is better disposed. I warn you now that if I can't obtain some useful information from those two men I'll be forced to begin questioning not only you and Mr Bold but also your daughters and Dr Grantly. Someone here must know something about this murder!'

Mr Harding let Mrs Winthrop escort the inspector out of the house. While she was doing that he sat motionless on the chair in his study. Then slowly but surely he began to make all the moves associated with playing the violincello. With one hand he made the slightest possible passes with an imaginary fiddle bow and with the fingers of the other he stopped sundry imaginary strings. This was a practice that he engaged in whenever he was highly agitated. The more vexed he was the shorter and slower would be the passes and the upper hand would not be seen to work. Only when his mind began to see a way through the problem would he rise to a higher melody. Then he would sweep the unseen strings with a bolder hand, and swiftly finger the chords from his neck, down along his waistcoat, and up again to his ear. On this occasion he could see no way out of his problems and so he continued performing on his imaginary violincello until interrupted by the entrance of Trollope into the study.

Trollope was upset to see how badly the warden was taking what had happened. He looked like a man who was experiencing nothing but suffering: it was evident in his tightened mouth and trouble-laden eyes. 'Now that the interviews are over for today, is there anything more I can do for you, Mr Harding?' he asked kindly.

'I wish you could but I fear that I'll find no comfort until we've discovered who was responsible for poor Thomas's death.'

Instinctively Trollope tried to divert the poor man's attention on to something other than the bedesman's death. 'Would you mind telling me a little about Barchester as I'm new here?' he suggested.

The warden was at first surprised that a man could think of such matters at such a time but, seeing the concern in Trollope's face, he recognized the motivation that lay behind the question. This was no ill-timed idle curiosity. It was an attempt to turn the focus of his mind on to less painful images. 'Barchester's origin lies in the fact several ancient trade routes used to cross this region and a hill fort was created to serve as a market place in times of peace and a stronghold in times of strife. The fort was subsequently developed first by the Romans, then by the Saxons, and finally by the Normans, who built not only a motte and bailey castle on its site but also a cathedral.'

'Presumably the precursor of the current building?'

'No, not quite. In the thirteenth century the Church decided to create a new cathedral outside the castle at the confluence of the Avon and the Nadder and it was round this that the new town of Barchester developed.'

'And has the cathedral changed much in the intervening centuries?'

'The only major change has been the creation of its wonderful spire in the fourteenth century. By that time Barchester had developed into one of the largest and richest cities in the country because of its importance in the wool trade.'

Trollope saw that the warden was taking no pleasure in their discussion, but decided to persevere with it. 'I saw no evidence of that wool trade today,' he said in a tone that invited a further response.

'No, the city's merchants failed to rise to the challenge of changing fashions. Fortunately in the seventeenth century the city found a new role as a centre for those wishing to visit Stonehenge. Barchester became known for its flannels, serges, blanketings, linseys, cottons and fancy cloths, and for some other high-quality goods. Sadly, it's no longer fashionable to come here but the evidence of the city's former wealth abounds in the many old buildings that you saw today.'

'I can see why their beauty has kept you here.'

For the first time Trollope's words seemed to touch the warden and make him forget the tragedy that had torn apart the community he served. His face ceased to look quite so careworn. 'It's another beauty that has made me so happy here. Planning the worship at the cathedral has been a source of constant joy to me.'

What more might have been said was prevented by the arrival of Mrs Winthrop with the news that the warden's daughters and son-in-law had returned to Hiram's Hospital. At once the warden's face returned to its former troubled state. What was he to say to his daughters about what had happened? And what would his son-in-law have to say? The murder was bound to bring the almshouse into disrepute. His misery took visible shape once again in the momentary clutching for a violincello that did not exist. Trollope moved to leave, judging that the warden would prefer to meet his family without having a stranger present. However, his exit from the study was prevented by the unexpectedly quick appearance of Eleanor Harding.

'What's wrong, Papa?' she asked, rushing across to her father. 'Something terrible has obviously happened in our absence.'

Trollope thought Mr Harding's daughter was very striking. She was not beautiful in the classical sense because she lacked the pearly white skin tone and the finely chiselled features and the perfection of shape associated with that. What she had instead was a radiant personality that exuded affection and warmth. Almost instantaneously Trollope decided that here was a woman whom you might pass in the street without notice, but whom you could hardly pass an evening with and not lose your heart. He could not help smiling. It was no wonder that John Bold was a constant visitor to the hospital!

Mr Harding greeted the emotional arrival of his daughter with a degree of reserve that sprang from his natural shyness but Trollope could see the natural affection that existed between them. However, before the warden could say anything, his other daughter also entered the room. She looked ten years older than her sister although maybe marriage and bringing up children had aged her. She lacked Eleanor's vivacity, but she had a good-natured face and a pleasing figure. Trollope thought that he detected in her manner a steadiness that many men would find attractive, especially if they had lost a wife and were looking for another who would care for their children.

Her husband, the Rev. Dr Theophilus Grantly, followed her into the room. He looked quite a few years older than her but he was a good-looking man with heavy eyebrows, large open eyes and a full mouth and chin. Trollope could see at once that he was the polar opposite in terms of temperament to Mr Harding. If the warden was a model of Christian meekness, Dr Grantly was the personification of the Church militant. He wore his broad-brimmed hat, his fine frock coat, his decorous breeches and his neat black gaiters as if they were the armour of God. Why had the young Susan Harding agreed to marry such a formidable figure, especially as it committed her to caring for five children? Was it genuine love or had she been won over by his status and what he could do for her father's career?

Mr Harding seemed to draw strength from the presence of his family and his initial confusion quickly vanished. Although his voice shook a little, he introduced Trollope to his family and then proceeded to inform them of the murder that had taken place and the resulting visit of the police inspector. The more Mr Harding spoke the unhappier Dr Grantly became. He was annoyed that his father-in-law had not immediately tried to send word to him of what had happened and angry to hear that the inspector had made so little progress in solving the case. Nor was he happy about his father-in-law offering accommodation to a stranger, though he could not say that in Trollope's presence.

'I really don't know where to begin,' he grunted when Mr Harding had ceased his tale. 'You should have sent for me straightaway and let me deal with the police. Don't you realize the danger this story poses to the reputation of the almshouse if the killer is not swiftly found? Once the profane press get hold of what has happened they'll produce the most lurid accounts. The adverse publicity could permanently damage the reputation of Hiram's Hospital.'

'I'm sorry, Archdeacon. I think the shock prevented me thinking clearly on the matter,' Mr Harding replied penitently.

The apology did not appease Dr Grantly. 'I should also add that I think John Bold's involvement in today's events is very undesirable,' he said angrily. 'I know you've liked him since the days when he sat as a boy and listened to your playing, but now he's a dangerous firebrand. He's always going on about the need for the Church to reform itself.'

'That's only because he loves the Church and wants it to play an even greater role in society.'

'As far as I'm concerned, he has all the fervour of a revolutionary and we all know what excesses that led to in France!'

This attack on John Bold did not please Eleanor Harding but she was too frightened of her brother-in-law to openly challenge him. Instead she tried to change the subject by pointing out how exhausted her poor father was.

Mrs Grantly graciously supported her sister by seeking to divert the conversation. 'I don't suppose either Papa or Mr Trollope has eaten properly for the day,' she said calmly and with an authority of manner that brooked no denial. 'I want to hear no more about this sordid matter until they have both had some nourishment. Eleanor, why don't you go to the kitchen and ask Mrs Winthrop to arrange for supper to be served as soon as possible in the dining room. While that's happening, may I suggest, dearest husband, you stay here with Papa so you can together write a letter that can be sent to your father informing him of what's happened here. I know the bishop is too unwell at present to come to the hospital but he'll be able to ensure that the police are guarded in what information they supply to the press. As for myself, I would ask, Mr Trollope, that you accompany me into the drawing room. There you can tell me a little more about yourself. It'll help take my mind off what's happened.'

Although the archdeacon controlled many things in the church, it was his wife who held the mastery in matters domestic and everyone did as they were bid. Trollope followed Mrs Grantly into the parlour but not without some nervousness. He quite rightly suspected that she wanted an opportunity to find out whether her father's trust in him might be justified. He was suddenly acutely conscious that he was only wearing what he had worn to travel to Barchester and that his dusty and dirty garments did little to enhance his position.

'How did you end up working for the Post Office, Mr Trollope?' Mrs Grantly asked once she had made herself comfortable and directed him to a nearby chair. Her mouth pursed slightly and she raised her eyebrows as she looked at him. 'It's an unusual profession for a gentleman.'

'That's a long story, Mrs Grantly, and I'm not sure you would want to hear it all. Suffice it to say that for financial reasons my parents moved abroad when I was nineteen and a friend of the family found me employment in London at the Post Office.'

Her face retained its solemn manner. 'And do you enjoy your work?' she enquired.

Trollope looked at her astute face and judged that she would be better won over by total honesty than by any attempt to gloss over his life. 'I confess that I hated it at first and for seven years my life was neither creditable to myself nor useful to the public service. I got into debt through spending too much time gambling and I acquired a reputation for being insubordinate and unpunctual. In the end my supervisor, a man called Maberley, got rid of me by packing me off to a post in Banagher in County Offaly in Ireland. I think he thought it would be the end of me but in fact it gave me a new start and now I love my work.'

'And may I ask what led to this transformation?'

'Mainly that my work in Ireland was far more enjoyable. Instead of being chained to a desk I spent most of my time outdoors on horseback and met with all kinds of people from lowly cottagers to grand landowners. I also found that my circumstances were much improved because my salary went much farther in Ireland than it had in London and I met the young woman who eventually became my wife. To win her father's approval I had to show that I could be a worthy husband. The rest you know from what Mr Harding has already told you about me. I am currently working on improving the postal routes in the southwest of England.'

Mrs Grantly's intuition told her that he had spoken the truth. Her alarm at finding her father had invited a stranger to stay began to ebb away. 'And do you have ambitions to do anything else?' she enquired.

Trollope blushed. 'I would like to become a successful author like my mother. Perhaps you've heard of her?'

'Surely you don't mean that Fanny Trollope is your mother?' gasped Mrs Grantly.

'Yes, she is.'

'I read her first book on the domestic manners of Americans with huge delight and since then I have read quite a few of her other travel books and all of her novels. They're very good.' She looked at Trollope with fresh interest. 'Have you yet had anything published?'

'I have but not to great success. A few years ago I had a three-volume novel called *The Macdermots of Ballycloran* published but it was not well received in England. If I'm honest, I think it was only published in the first place because the printer hoped people would see the name "Trollope" and think my mother had written it. I tried again with a novel called *The Kellys and the O'Kellys* but hardly anyone bothered purchasing it. After that my publisher told me he could give me no further encouragement to write.'

'I'm not sure that any author would find it easy to win popularity by setting his novels in Ireland,' Mrs Grantly commented. She made the country sound as if it created a bad taste in her mouth. 'You should have chosen a more congenial setting for your books.'

Trollope tried not to show his amusement. He was used to those who knew nothing of Ireland maligning it. 'I did try my hand at historical fiction. I wrote a book on the French Revolution called *La Vendée*. It also was not a success.'

'If you'll pardon me for saying so, I don't think writing about that horrid revolution was any more sensible a choice! Perhaps you should write society novels. That's what your mother excels at.'

'You may be right but I've not wished to directly compete with her books.'

'A laudable desire but I doubt whether your mother

would worry about that if it meant her son achieved success,' she replied with a twinkle of amusement in her eyes.

'You may well be right, Mrs Grantly,' he answered tactfully.

Their conversation was interrupted by a polite knock on the door and the housekeeper entered to announce that supper was ready. Mrs Grantly at once rose from her chair and offered to escort Trollope to the dining room where Eleanor Harding was already awaiting them. Once Mr Harding and Dr Grantly joined them, they all sat down to eat. Trollope could not help noticing how finely the room was furnished and how the table was laid with fine silver tableware. Surely the philanthropist John Hiram had never intended his bequest to result in the warden living in such splendour? Mrs Winthrop had prepared a meal that would have made even the most determined observer of Lent surrender to temptation, but the events of the day cast such a shadow over the proceedings that none of them ate very much. Nevertheless, they pretended to enjoy what they were eating and they engaged in polite conversation. In that process Mrs Grantly shared with the others what she had learned about Trollope's literary ambitions and his connection to the famous writer, Mrs Fanny Trollope.

When they had all finished their pretence at eating, Mrs Grantly sent for Mrs Winthrop and asked her to commence clearing away the unwanted food and to bring some port. Whilst this was happening, the archdeacon requested a far more detailed account of what the bedesmen had said to the inspector during their interrogation. Mr Harding duly obliged. Trollope listened with particular interest because it was his first opportunity to find out what he had missed by not being present during the interviews. Everyone listened very intently, even the housekeeper, who appeared to take more time over her task than was necessary. The only interruption took place when Mr Harding told them what Abel Handy had said.

'How dare the man insinuate that one of us might be responsible!' stormed Dr Grantly. 'He should be horsewhipped for his impudence! I seem to recall that I told you at the time that he shouldn't be admitted to this hospital. He's a born troublemaker!'

What more might have been said was prevented by a knock on the front door that heralded the arrival of Trollope's baggage. He immediately requested that he should be permitted to go to his room to unpack and attend to his ablutions before retiring for the night. The others readily assented to this and his departure acted as a catalyst for the meeting to break up.

'I think Eleanor and I would also benefit from going upstairs to our respective rooms. I feel in need of a rest and I'm sure she does too,' announced Mrs Grantly.

'I think that would do both of you good,' concurred Mr Harding. 'I think that I'll go for a short walk in the garden before I go to bed. I may also use the opportunity to visit some of the bedesmen to see how they are faring. It has been remiss of me not to visit them all. Do you wish to accompany me, Archdeacon?'

'No, I'm sure you do not require my assistance. I would prefer to retire back into your study because I've some urgent ecclesiastical papers that require my attention before I go to bed.'

As Trollope made his way upstairs to his room, he found himself thinking about what Abel Handy had said. Someone had plunged a knife into Thomas Rider with unerring precision. Did that not point to a younger and firmer hand wielding the weapon? Most of the bedesmen were far too frail. The trouble was that he could not see any of the Harding family committing such a crime. None of them had any motive to kill Thomas Rider. Nor did any of them look like the kind of person who would commit such a crime. Mr Harding was far too kind, and his daughters both appeared to be fine women in their own respective ways. It was equally difficult to see Dr Grantly as a killer. He might be a bit pompous but Trollope suspected his heart was in the right place. That left only John Bold, but he also appeared to be a very good man. The more Trollope thought about it, the more impossible the whole thing seemed. The old men who might possibly have some hidden reason for killing Rider lacked the physical capacity to do so, while those at Hiram's Hospital who were fit enough to commit the murder had neither the reason nor temperament to do it. Yet someone had stabbed the man that morning. Who could it possibly be? And for what possible motive?

4

ANOTHER MURDER

It WAS ABOUT an hour after breakfast on the following morning that Inspector Blake returned. Mrs Winthrop showed him into the warden's study. There Dr Grantly received him but without any sign of welcome. Standing with his back to the empty fireplace, the archdeacon immediately began lecturing him on the importance of making sure that the case was handled with the utmost discretion. 'My father-in-law is a shy and retiring man, Mr Blake. He takes comfort in the quiet obscurity of this place. I must therefore ask you to take great care in whatever statements you make to the press. There are too many journalists who think it's their role to criticize anything to do with the Church and you know as well as I do that they'll seize on this murder and will milk it for all it's worth. They'll sensationalize the manner of Thomas Rider's death and then accuse Mr Harding of failing to protect the residents here.'

'I understand your concern, sir, but controlling what the press says is not within my power.'

The archdeacon threw up his arms in disgust. 'No, but you can seek to ensure that silly speculation is suppressed by not listening to the nonsense that has been spouted by men like Abel Handy. If he thinks for one moment that he has your ear, he'll be spewing his venom to any reporter prepared to listen to him.'

'I'm aware that Mr Handy's comments have already caused Mr Harding distress, but it's my role to leave no stone unturned. A man has been murdered and his blood cries out for justice. I'll not rest till the murderer is brought to trial.'

'But that doesn't mean having to treat everyone as a suspect. What Abel Handy told you yesterday was a damned impertinence!' He glowered at Blake. 'I trust you'll not follow up his malicious nonsense.'

The inspector's eyes widened at this challenge to his authority. 'I'll have to pursue every line of enquiry until the identity of the murderer is uncovered,' he replied firmly.

'I didn't take you for a fool, sir, but I tell you only a fool would consider for a moment that any member of this family would stoop so low as to become involved in a murder. The very idea is preposterous! I think I speak for the bishop when I say that we'll not have you treat the members of this family like suspects.'

'Is that a threat, Dr Grantly?'

The archdeacon stared at him, his face twisted with temper. 'You can call it whatever you wish, sir. I simply say it would be unwise for you to offend those who have access to your superiors. I hope you agree with me.'

Blake's face reddened and he clenched hold of the

top of the chair that stood in front of him. 'With all due respect, sir, you can't expect me not to ask questions of the family. That process doesn't mean that I believe one of you may be guilty. I simply think that one of you might be able to shed light on a possible motive for the murder. If we know the motive we'll know the killer.'

These words failed to satisfy the archdeacon. 'If we knew anything, sir, we would speak without having to be questioned. I want your word that you'll leave us entirely out of your interrogations!'

'Reflect on what you say, Dr Grantly. I think the newspapers wouldn't take kindly to any hint that simple police enquiries are being prevented.' These words visibly shook the archdeacon, who recognized the threat implicit in them. Blake would use the press against them if pushed too far. Fortunately for Dr Grantly, the inspector chose not to pursue his new-found advantage because he lacked any evidence to support Abel Handy's accusation. 'Please don't press me too hard, sir,' he continued. 'Rest assured that I'll do nothing lightly in this matter. At present I've not even made the press aware of the murder. I'll give you and the bishop suitable notice of whatever I intend to do in my investigation.'

Dr Grantly saw an olive leaf was being proffered and responded accordingly. 'That's all I ask, Inspector,' he said with as much charm as he could muster in the circumstances. 'Perhaps you would share with me your current thinking on who might be the murderer?'

'At first I thought it might have been Mr Trollope but I'm almost certain now that he's just an innocent bystander. I've yet to have his identity verified by the Post Office in London but I've no reason to believe he is lying to us. What information I've gleaned from his groom confirms that he's been undertaking surveying work in the area and that he arrived in Barchester only yesterday. I can see no reason why he would kill an old man whom he had never met before.'

'I agree. My wife has ascertained he comes from a respectable family. He's the son of the novelist Fanny Trollope.'

The inspector almost said that respectability was no guarantee of innocence but fortunately stopped himself in time. It would only have rekindled the archdeacon's anger. Instead he switched the conversation to safer ground. 'One of the bedesmen must be our killer, but I confess, Dr Grantly, I've no clues yet as to which of them it is or the motive for the crime.'

'If I were a betting man my money would be on Abel Handy,' replied the archdeacon. 'The man should never have been made a bedesman in the first place. He's a known troublemaker!'

'I've no time for the man but he's far too crippled to be our murderer,' Blake countered. 'Let us hope that we can persuade Jeremiah Smith and John Gaunt to reveal what they know.'

'If I'd been present at your questioning I wouldn't have permitted Smith to leave the study without telling you everything he knew. Nor would I have let John Gaunt stay in his room. Mr Harding is too soft in his dealings with the bedesmen. In my experience such men see kindness as mere weakness.'

Blake declined to comment. Though he had been

cross the previous day, he knew which of the two clergymen he preferred and he was confident that it would be Smith's respect for Mr Harding that would lead him to speak rather than fear of the archdeacon. Whether he was right in this assessment was not tested because at that moment the warden burst into the study. His face was as white as a newly laundered sheet. 'Jeremiah has been murdered!' he exclaimed. 'I went to visit him in his room in order to make sure that he would tell us whatever he knew, but when I knocked at his door there was no answer. When I entered—' He stopped speaking and struggled to control his emotion. His hand wavered as if about to seek his imaginary violincello, but then he mastered himself and resumed his account. 'I found him lying dead on the floor in a pool of his own blood. He's been stabbed in the chest like poor Thomas.'

Blake was the first to recover from the shock. 'Was there any sign of a struggle?'

'None.' He shuddered as the image of what he had seen flashed forcefully across his mind, and added in a low whisper, 'I felt his lifeless eyes accuse me for having failed to protect him. If only I'd persuaded him to tell us what he knew last night he might still be alive.'

'Take us to the body,' said Dr Grantly.

The warden immediately led the way. En route they met Anthony Trollope emerging from the drawing room and they informed him of what had happened. He joined them in going to Smith's room. The warden could not bring himself to re-enter the scene of the crime and when the three other men saw the body they could understand why. It was sprawled across the floor and there was a wide circle of blood all around it. The inspector shook his head from side to side. 'The murderer realized that he needed to silence this man. Do you agree, Dr Grantly?'

'That would seem the logical conclusion to draw.'

'In which case, it proves our killer is not some stranger but a person who knows exactly what is going on within the hospital.'

'You're right, Inspector,' interjected Trollope. 'And the location of this second murder points to the same conclusion. I don't believe that any stranger could have found his way into this dead man's room unnoticed. Not with all the bedesmen aware of what had just happened to Thomas Rider. I think Smith knew his killer and had no suspicions in letting him enter his home. That's why there's no sign of any conflict. He may even have invited him here in order to clarify whether he had behaved rightly or wrongly in holding back information from you.'

'Then he paid dearly for his naivety!' muttered the inspector. He turned towards Dr Grantly, who had remained silent throughout this exchange. 'Sir, I want you to inform the housekeeper what's happened and tell her to ensure that this room is kept locked until Mr Bold is brought here. I want him to undertake a medical examination of the body as soon as possible.'

Dr Grantly's brow instantly furrowed. 'Surely Mr Bold is not the right choice of doctor?' he queried.

'I disagree, sir. Mr Bold was the doctor who examined Thomas Rider and therefore I judge he is the doctor best placed to compare whether the hand that killed him is also the hand that has slain Jeremiah Smith.' The tone with which he said this showed he was not prepared to change his mind. 'Mr Harding will have more than enough to do informing the ladies about what's happened and fetching Mr Bold, so I suggest, Dr Grantly, that you and I begin the process of interviewing the bedesmen. I got nowhere yesterday but I'm convinced some of them must know what lies behind these murders. I assume, Mr Trollope, that you are willing to assist Mrs Winthrop in bringing the old men one by one to Mr Harding's study so we can again interview them? '

'Certainly but what do you wish us to say to each man before we bring them into your presence? Do we inform them about this second murder?'

'Yes, you should,' replied Blake. 'But don't dwell on the details of how he was killed. If one of them is the killer then we can perhaps trick him into revealing that by showing some knowledge of the means of murder.'

'Do you want to see John Gaunt first?'

'Yes. He's now our best hope. It's just possible that he may know what is going on here. And, if he doesn't, he may yet say things that will help guide my questions to the others. As far as the rest are concerned, they can come in any order. You don't need to stick to yesterday's pattern.'

Over the next hour or so the second round of questioning of Gaunt and the others proved as abortive as the first. All found it incomprehensible that two murders should have taken place within the sanctity of their home at Hiram's Hospital. It was as if all the certainty of their existence had been lost and not just two of their number. The last to be seen was Jonathan Crumple and Mrs Winthrop asked Trollope to help the bedesman back to his room. He was doing this when John Bold arrived at the almshouse. Crumple recoiled from the doctor as if he were avoiding a snake and hurried to get into the safety of his room. Trollope followed him and shut the door. He could see the old man was deeply troubled about something. In as kind a voice as he could muster, he tried to tease out the reason.

'It's nothing, sir. I'm just grieving over what 'as 'appened 'ere,' mumbled the bedesman and he wiped his mouth nervously with the back of his gnarled hand.

'That's perfectly understandable. Both Mr Rider and Mr Smith were your friends.'

A flush of embarrassment spread across Crumble's withered cheeks. 'Aye, they were, and what's bothering me is what I saw,' he whispered, anxious not to be overheard.

'What you saw? Then tell me about it, Mr Crumple.'

The bedesman shook his head. 'I don't think that would be right, sir. That's why I said nothing to the inspector or the archdeacon just now.'

' Why not?'

'I've nothing against 'em or you, Mr Trollope. It's just I'm not sure that I want what I saw to be known by all. It would cause pain to Mr Harding and I may be wrong in thinking it 'as anything to do with the murders. Indeed, I 'ope I am.'

Trollope's mind raced. Could it be that Crumble had

the evidence to identify the murderer? And why should the murderer's identity cause pain to Mr Harding unless it was a member of his family? Or perhaps John Bold? He knew that he had somehow to persuade the bedesman to speak out. 'Surely you must see that you owe it to your dead friends to tell us what you saw?'

Tears filled the old man's eyes and he bowed his head. His whole body began to shake as he sobbed. 'I can't. I can't. Mr Harding would nivver forgive me.'

'Tell me, Mr Crumple, what you saw,' said Trollope in a firm but kind voice. 'Let me judge its importance. I promise you I'll repeat nothing to anyone else without your permission.' He sat down next to the bedesman and, stretching out his left arm, placed it around the old man's shoulder. 'Come now, a trouble shared is a trouble halved. Tell me what you know. It may be that you are worrying yourself needlessly.'

This last comment seemed to strike home and, after a show of reluctance, Crumple whispered what he had seen into Trollope's ear. 'I 'appened to look out of my window on the morning that Thomas Rider was killed and I saw Mr Bold 'iding in the bushes that grow near to the warden's house. Miss Harding came out and spoke with 'im. I've no idea what they said but she seemed very agitated and he appeared to be trying to calm her down. I was curious so I left my room and made my way towards 'em. As I drew nearer, I 'eard Miss Harding say, "I'll not stand for this! Something must be done to stop 'im!" I didn't catch Mr Bold's reply but she muttered something about 'ow it would be difficult to see 'im again that evening. At that moment she ran off and I saw there were tears in 'er eyes. I walked on but by the time I reached the place where they'd met Mr Bold wasn't there. I think 'e must have gone in the opposite direction.'

'Why did you not tell this to the inspector yesterday?' enquired Trollope.

'I didn't connect what I'd seen with Thomas's death.'

'But now you think that's possible, so why have you still not told the inspector?'

'It's not for me to tell Miss Harding's business to the police. It's up to 'er if she wants to tell 'em about what she were doing with Mr Bold.'

'You know very well that she's not going to do that if she and John Bold were plotting Thomas Rider's death. And, if they are innocent, there's no reason for you to fear anyone investigating the matter. I think you should've told the inspector and archdeacon what you've told me.' The old man's face was pitiable in its agony. He looked deeply miserable. Trollope sensed that he had not yet told him everything. 'What made you change your mind about the significance of their meeting?' he asked.

Crumple looked nervously all around him, his hunched shoulders and clenched hands indicating how tense he was. 'I 'ad a very unsettled night last night and I woke just after dawn,' he said, nervously licking his dry lips. 'When I looked out of my window I again saw Miss Harding out early. This time she were walking outside the almshouse in her nightclothes. She could easily have come from seeing Jeremiah.'

Trollope was rendered speechless by this second revelation. Could it really be the case that Eleanor Harding was the murderer? If she was not, then what possessed her to be out walking undressed in the early hours of the morning? It was an unlikely hour for her to be keeping a second assignation with Bold.

Now that he had admitted what he had seen, Crumple babbled on. 'What if I'm wrong, sir, in thinking there's something bad in 'er actions? By saying what I saw I'd have ruined 'er reputation. Just imagine what the gossips of Barchester would make of it!'

Trollope knew the bedesman was right. Eleanor Harding would be crucified if such information leaked out. The scandal of a young woman meeting a man in the bushes and wandering about undressed in the early hours of the morning would destroy not only her reputation but that of the entire Harding family. The clerical careers of both Mr Harding and Dr Grantly would be instantly shattered. Yet what Crumple had seen could not be simply swept under the carpet. What if she and Bold were behind the murders? He struggled to know what to say and then came up with the one way forward that might enable an investigation whilst still protecting her.

He put a hand under Crumple's chin and firmly lifted his head so that he could look him fully in the face. 'I think you may have been right not to speak to the inspector or Dr Grantly, but you should tell Mr Harding,' he said in as authoritative a voice as he could manage. 'He's her father and he has a right to know and to decide what to do with the information.'

A look of panic flashed across the bedesman's face. 'But he might think that I've been spying on 'is daughter. Then he'd be very displeased with me, sir.'

'A father would want to know what you saw. Let Mr

Harding decide what he does with the information.'

'I can't tell 'im, sir. I can't. I wouldn't be able to bear seeing the pain in 'is eyes.'

'Then let me tell him what you saw,' Trollope commanded. He saw from the expression on Crumple's face that the man was wavering and added, 'I need not tell him that the source of the information was you. I'll say that a bedesman told me in the strictest confidence and asked not to be named. Does that not satisfy your concerns?'

The old man still trembled but he weakly nodded his assent and Trollope immediately left to fulfil his new task. He knew that both the inspector and Dr Grantly were intending to join John Bold in the latest victim's room. As a consequence he had every chance of catching Mr Harding alone in his study. As he walked towards the warden's house, he wished that he were not the bearer of such bad news. The evidence against Eleanor Harding and John Bold was circumstantial but it looked damning. What if Mr Harding could offer no evidence to show their innocence? Trollope did not feel he would then be able to keep his promise of confidentiality. He would have to inform the inspector so a full investigation could take place rather than risk letting a murderer escape justice. How would the warden view such a betrayal from a man to whom he had offered hospitality? He was so lost in his thoughts that it was not until he reached the house that he realized Eleanor Harding was blocking his entrance to it.

'Mr Trollope, can you tell me what's going on?' she enquired. 'I understand why my father is distraught at having two murders here, but why is Mr Blake now seeking to question my sister and me about the matter?' She blushed as she went on to say, 'Surely we are not suspects?'

'My dear Miss Harding, I hope not,' prevaricated Trollope. 'I'm sure that Mr Blake is simply doing what's expected of him when two men have been murdered.'

'But both my sister and I were away with Dr Grantly when the first murder occurred and in our beds when the second took place. We can offer the inspector no information on either crime.'

Trollope was uncertain whether to confront her with what he knew or not. 'It's not as straightforward as that,' he said grimly.

'I don't understand what you mean.'

'It's possible that Mr Rider was murdered before you and your sister left here. The inspector is therefore bound to ask you about your movements yesterday morning.' He hesitated, still unsure whether he should say any more, and then said in a measured voice, 'I'm sure that your answers will have put him at ease about your innocence.' He saw from her face that this had not been the police response and decided to give her at least the opportunity to clarify what she had been doing that morning. 'As to this morning you were up very early – I know that because you were seen walking in your nightdress in the garden – so you might possibly have seen something that might help the inspector.'

Eleanor Harding's cheeks turned a deep red. Shame filled her face as she replied, 'I've no recollection of going outside my room.'

'But you must have!'

'No. I assure you I've none.' She saw the disbelief in his face and he saw her chew at her lips with her small pearl-white teeth. 'You think I'm lying, sir, but I'm not.' She spoke haltingly. Her voice sounded strained. 'If I did leave my room I was asleep at the time.'

'How can that be?' he asked incredulously.

'My father will tell you that I've been an occasional sleepwalker since I was a child and, when that happens, I remember nothing of what I did or where I went.'

Her confession threw a totally different complexion on the situation and Trollope was deeply embarrassed that she had been made to confide her weakness to a stranger like himself. 'I'm truly sorry to hear that you suffer from somnambulism,' he said apologetically. 'Can nothing be done about it?'

'My father has tried various doctors but their treatments have proved ineffective.'

'Then I'm sure that Inspector Blake will be understanding over the matter.'

'I wish that I had your confidence.' Her voice trembled. 'I fear it's more likely that he will assume my sleepwalking is an excuse to hide from him what I was really doing.'

'Then the sooner we can all get to the truth of what happened, the sooner the inspector will no longer have reason to question you,' Trollope replied ambiguously.

'And are you active in investigating the matter?'

'Not officially, Miss Harding. But I've a vested interest in finding out the truth because I don't think Mr Blake will let me leave Barchester until the murders are solved. I'm therefore talking to the bedesmen in the hope that one of them may say something to me that has not been said to the inspector. Many working men have a deep distrust of the police.'

'And has any of them said anything different to you?'

For a moment Trollope wanted to tell her the rest of what he had been told. Only the fact that he had promised Crumple not to reveal the source of his information prevented him. Instead he chose his words carefully. 'I've been told a number of things by different bedesmen, but I've nothing as yet that I can take to the inspector.'

He saw Miss Harding's lips tremble again. Was that relief that there was no evidence yet pointing to her involvement with John Bold? Or was it disappointment that he had as yet found nothing to prove her innocence? He could not judge. His senses told him that he was looking at a pure young lady but why, if that was the case, had she been skulking in bushes talking with the surgeon? And why could she not remember her movements that morning? Was her talk of sleepwalking the truth or was it just a convenient cover?

'I'm going out for a walk,' she said. 'I need some fresh air. Could you tell my father that I'm in the garden if he requires me?'

'Most certainly, Miss Harding, but where is he?'

'In his study. The inspector and Dr Grantly have gone to talk with Mr Bold. They think he will have finished his examination of the body by now. My father was too upset to accompany them.'

Once she had left, Trollope knocked at the oaken

door of the study. He heard the warden's voice say 'Come in,' and he entered.

'I'm sorry to intrude on you, Mr Harding, but I seem to have uncovered a rather disquieting event and I think you should be the first to hear about it. From my conversations with the bedesmen it would appear that one of them saw your daughter, Miss Eleanor, walking outside in her nightclothes this morning, although she has no memory of that.'

The warden gave a deep groan. 'I fear the murder has triggered an attack of the condition I had hoped was gone forever. As a child my daughter often sleep-walked but she has not done so for many years.'

Trollope was relieved to hear confirmation of what Eleanor had told him, but he knew he had yet to voice the more damming evidence against her. 'Unfortunately, Mr Harding, she was also seen holding a meeting with Mr Bold in the bushes outside your house yesterday morning.'

This time the warden did not immediately speak and it was obvious that the news caused him distress. Trollope quickly proceeded to outline what Crumple had seen and heard but without divulging the source. Mr Harding listened with increasing disapproval. 'And why has the person who saw this not reported the matter to the inspector?' he asked.

'He feared the inspector might misconstrue the nature of their meeting and that the story might be leaked to the outside world, damaging your family's reputation. The bedesman concerned loves you very much, Mr Harding, and he's kept quiet to avoid giving you any pain.'

Mr Harding was not naïve enough to be deluded as to what lay behind Trollope's visit. 'But he – and you – fear my daughter may be complicit in the deaths that have taken place and so you come to me,' he said with a quiver of his lips.

'You must recognize, Mr Harding, that it is a most unfortunate coincidence that her movements place her in a position where she could have killed both men.'

'How dare you or anyone even think for a moment that Eleanor might be involved in these crimes! She would not hurt a fly!'

'But what about Mr Bold?'

The warden wrung his hands with frustration. 'You wouldn't say that if you knew him. John may be a bit headstrong at times but, believe me, he's a very fine young man.'

'That's not what Dr Grantly thinks,' replied Trollope hastily.

'I'm afraid the archdeacon is prone to make rash judgements on people. He thinks Mr Bold lacking in wisdom and prudence because he will not believe all that Mr Grantly believes. That doesn't make Mr Bold a probable murderer! As a doctor he devotes his time to saving life, not destroying it. I've known him put his own life at risk on many an occasion because he would insist on treating those with contagious diseases.'

'Then why does Mr Grantly not respect him more, even if their opinions differ?' challenged Trollope.

'Because Mr Bold is a man of the people in every sense of that. He fights their cause. He has witnessed such poverty that he cannot abide the injustices within our society. That makes him an outspoken critic of anything he judges wrong, including some things within the Church.'

Trollope felt his pulse racing with the adrenalin of the moment, but realized that everything the warden said rang true. 'I accept all that you say, Mr Harding. I've no reason to doubt the good character of either your daughter or Mr Bold from my dealings with them. However, some might judge their meeting to be at best inappropriate and at worst a sign of some form of plotting.'

Colour burned up the warden's cheeks. 'I agree their behaviour was injudicious but I suspect I'm to blame for that.'

'In what way?'

'John and his sister Mary spent many a day here as they grew up. I loved the lad and increasingly saw him as being the son I never had. As a consequence it's not surprising that John became great friends with Eleanor and Susan. Sadly Susan's relationship with Dr Grantly led to her distancing herself from John, but that made Eleanor spring increasingly to his defence. The more she defended him, the more she found herself dwelling on his qualities as a man – and, of course, the more he appreciated her. For some time I've feared that the two of them may have fallen in love.'

'But if you like Mr Bold, why should that be a problem?'

Mr Harding breathed in deeply and sighed. 'Because of my son-in-law's antagonism to him. The harmony of my household would be ruined if John sought to marry Eleanor.'

Trollope frowned. 'Surely you would not deny

Eleanor happiness with a man she loves?'

'Not by choice. That's why I haven't denied John Bold access to this house even though Dr Grantly has long wanted me to do so. What I have done is prevent Eleanor and John from having opportunity to show affection towards each other. I hoped – perhaps foolishly – that I would be able to make my son-in-law eventually see the truth about John Bold's character.'

'What you're saying, Mr Harding, is that the family's attitude may explain why Eleanor and John Bold were meeting privately in the bushes?'

The warden nodded. 'I think my actions have made them resort to clandestine meetings.'

'But what about the overheard conversation between them? That was not talk of love but of action that was required against someone.'

'Eleanor may have been referring to me or to Dr Grantly.'

'That makes perfect sense but I doubt whether Mr Blake will accept your explanation of the purpose of their meeting. The information is likely to make them his prime suspects.'

'But they have no motive!'

'He will seek to find one.'

Mr Harding's normally benign face filled with anger. 'Then he'll be wasting his time!' He cleared his throat and then chose his next words carefully. 'We can only hope that Mr Blake does not get to hear about my daughter being outside this morning and about her meeting with Mr Bold yesterday. In that way he'll concentrate on other leads he may have acquired.'

Trollope knew he was standing at a crossroads. Mr

Harding was asking him to trust his version of events and to prevent the inspector hearing the bedesman's story. Dare he take such a risk? He thought once more about his first impressions of Eleanor Harding and John Bold. Could they really be guilty of two such horrendous crimes? And what possible motive could they have? Not without some disquietude he replied, 'I'll not tell the inspector anything.' He saw instant relief appear on the warden's face. 'I've no desire to provide information that would doubtless lead to two young people's reputation being needlessly dragged through the mud by the town gossips,' Trollope continued, 'but we must both pray that the true cause of these murders will soon be uncovered. I can't guarantee that my source may not also speak to others and the inspector may get to hear. If he does, both you and I will appear to have been deliberately hiding evidence from him. He won't like that!'

'I'll face that situation if it arises. In the interim I'm grateful for your understanding and for the concern shown by your informant in asking you to speak to me first. Pass on to him my thanks.'

5

THE SECRET OF CATHERINE FARRELL

WHEN TROLLOPE LEFT the warden's study he decided he might speak again with Miss Harding but he could see no sign of her in the garden. He therefore decided that he should return to Jonathan Crumple and encourage him to remain silent. However, as he entered the main door of the almshouse, he was diverted from this task by the sight of John Gaunt beckoning him to enter his room.

'Will you come in, Mr Trollope?' the old man asked plaintively. 'You were so very kind to me yesterday and I'm not sure who else I can turn to for advice.'

Trollope had been favourably impressed by the former gaoler the previous day, even though Gaunt had not been at his best because of his grief. He was better educated and better spoken than most of the other bedesmen and not at all the grim figure that Trollope had expected. 'If I can help, I certainly will,' he replied.

There was little in the way of comfort in Gaunt's room. The furniture was old and worn and the carpet had long lost its original colour and was threadbare. The sole decoration was a large cross that hung on one of the walls. Below this stood an old lectern on which rested an ancient copy of a Bible. Judging from its tatty appearance it had been much thumbed. Trollope sat down on a plain oak chair and Gaunt slowly lowered himself into another so the two men faced each other. There was a long pause because both looked for the other to speak first. Finally the bedesman nervously wiped the side of his face and his jaw with his left hand and then asked, 'Is there any chance that Jeremiah died a natural death?'

'No. He was definitely murdered.'

'Then am I right in thinking that none of us is safe until the murderer is found?'

'I'm afraid that may be the case.'

'But why should anyone choose to kill any of us? Each of us already has a foot in the grave. What's so urgent that we must be sent into the afterlife ahead of the limited time that we've left?'

Trollope sensed Gaunt was hiding something and wondered how best to draw him out. He hesitated and then replied, 'No one knows the murderer's motive but we know both Thomas Rider and Jeremiah Smith were privy to some secret. I think it's possible that they were killed because the murderer wanted to silence them. Do you agree?' He saw Gaunt visibly pale and hazarded a guess. 'Do you perhaps know the same secret? If you do, then you shouldn't require me to tell you that your life may also be at risk.'

'What I know may have nothing to do with their deaths,' countered Gaunt, unwittingly providing

Trollope with the knowledge that he was the holder of information.

Trollope pressed home his advantage. 'Or it may. Do you want to take that risk? Why not confide in me?'

Gaunt swallowed hard and fought back his tears. 'Because what I know concerns Mr Harding. I'd rather die than inflict any suffering on him.'

'He wouldn't wish for you to also die. Why don't you tell him what you know?'

Gaunt shuddered. 'He already knows.'

'Then tell me. I promise that I'll say nothing to the police. If I know what the secret is, then I can talk with Mr Harding and perhaps he and I can together resolve these murders.'

Like Crumple before him, Gaunt was clearly uncertain what to do, but his desire for self-preservation eventually won the day and he reluctantly muttered, 'Very well, Mr Trollope, I'll tell you what I fear and why I fear it, even though I remained silent when questioned by the inspector and the archdeacon.'

'I'm sure you've decided to do the right thing,' Trollope reassured.

The bedesman sighed. 'Only time will tell. You see, I've strong reason to believe that the killer must be one of Mr Harding's daughters.'

'Which one?'

'That I don't know, but Mr Harding will.'

'You are talking in riddles. Please explain!'

'The world thinks that Mr Harding has two daughters but in fact only one of them is truly his. The other is adopted and has tainted blood. I'm certain that she would do anything to keep secret her true ancestry!

92

I told Thomas Rider about it and I suspect he told Jeremiah, even though I told him to keep the information to himself. She must have discovered that they knew and she has silenced them.'

Trollope was staggered. Could there really be some dark family secret behind the murders? 'Tell me what you know and how you came to possess the information,' he commanded.

'My case is an unusual one,' commenced Gaunt, 'because I'm the only bedesman not to have lived and worked entirely in Barchester. I was born here but my parents died when I was still a young lad. I was sent to London to be brought up by my mother's sister and I returned to Barchester only about ten years or so ago when a protracted sickness forced me to abandon my work at Newgate Prison. And I bless the day that I came back because Mr Harding took pity on me and recommended that I should become a bedesman here. If not for his kindness I'd have ended up in the workhouse.' The thought of what might have happened to him was sufficient to deeply disturb Gaunt. He struggled to contain his feelings and it was a while before he felt able to resume his account. 'My apologies, sir,' he mumbled, 'I find it harder to hide my feelings now that I'm old.'

Trollope sought to reassure him. 'Don't fret, Mr Gaunt. Your feelings do you credit. Just take your time.'

'As a child I was happy in London. My aunt was a good woman and her husband treated me as if I were his son, though I was no blood relation. I think it helped that he'd no child of his own. They made sure that I received a good education both at school and in church. He worked as a turnkey at the Marshalsea and some days he would take me with him to the cells. I'd run errands for those prisoners who had the means to make their stay in prison more comfortable. I'd purchase what they required in return for a small fee.'

'Was that a safe thing for a young lad to do?'

Gaunt smiled at Trollope's ignorance. 'There was nothing to fear. The people I served were just in prison for debt. Such contact as I had with them served only to convince me never to become like them. I saw their misery and I vowed never to gamble or otherwise get into debt by borrowing. I've seen the suffering moneylenders cause. They seize on those in need and plunge them into even greater debt. I'm proud to say, sir, that I've kept my vow unbroken to this day. I've either gone without or saved until I could afford what I wanted. '

'I wish I could say the same,' replied Trollope ruefully. 'Unfortunately a few years ago I borrowed some money and fell into the hands of a moneylender. He made my life hell so I know exactly what you mean. Presumably you became a gaoler because you wished to follow in your uncle's footsteps?'

'Yes, but often I wish I'd not chosen Newgate. When I've a bad night here and can't get to sleep it's usually because something has triggered off memories of my time there. I saw some terrible sights, sir, the worst being the public hangings on Monday mornings. It wasn't just watching the condemned men and women go through all the agony of being hung. Far worse was seeing the faces of the scum who came to enjoy the spectacle. Sometimes as many as twenty thousand would gather, shouting and swearing and singing. 'Tis hard to believe this is supposed to be a Christian nation when one sees such a sight.'

A visible shudder passed through the old man's frame and Trollope could see Gaunt was reliving in his mind all the wicked behaviour that humans at their worst can show. Wanting to bring the old man's mind back to the present, he asked, 'But what's all this to do with events here?'

"'Twas at Newgate I first met Mr Harding.'

Trollope's mind reeled. Surely it was not possible that the kindly warden was a former felon? And if so, for what crime? Had he been imprisoned for debt or for some far worse act?

'He used to come on Sundays,' continued Gaunt, 'in order to preach from the pulpit in the prison chapel. Those condemned to death used to sit with their coffins in the large black pen built for that purpose below the reading desk.'

'Their coffins?' queried Trollope, relieved that his initial concern about the warden had been groundless.

'Yes. It doesn't happen now but it used to be the tradition that each person's coffin would be placed upon the seat by their side throughout the whole service.'

'I'd no idea that such an unnecessary act took place.'

'It was to bring home to the prisoners the fate they were about to face. That's also why the walls of the chapel were painted with religious texts about them having to face God's justice. Unlike some preachers, Mr Harding tried to offer them hope rather than condemning them. He preached of God's continued love for them and how, if they repented of the wrongs

95

they'd done, they'd be forgiven. He was very eloquent that morning and a couple of the condemned were sufficiently moved that they asked him to visit them in their cells. He promised that he would. That's how he came to know Catherine Farrell and I wish for his sake that meeting had not happened. You'll know why I say that when I tell what resulted from it.'

'Who was she?'

'A convicted murderess in her mid-twenties with the looks of an angel. I've never seen such a beautiful woman before or since. I tell you, sir, she had eyes that were the colour of cornflowers, a complexion that was as soft and white as rose petals, and hair as yellow as a buttercup. However, I knew from the reports of her trial that she was a most deceitful and wicked woman who showed no remorse for having killed her husband. No angel who fell from grace could've fallen as much as her.'

'What had led her to murder him?'

'From an early age she used her beauty to attract men and she eventually chose to marry the wealthiest of her suitors, a man called William Courtenay, the nephew of Lord Hazleworth and heir to his title. The jury was told he was a fine young man until he came under her influence. She encouraged him into a life of debauchery and, within a few years, drove him into bankruptcy through her wild excesses. Rather than relinquish her lifestyle she sought to seduce her husband's rich uncle and so gain access to his wealth. When she discovered that he was too virtuous to succumb to her evil charms, she resorted to another method. She said that she'd accuse Lord Hazleworth of raping her unless he immediately made over half his wealth to his nephew, However, her husband refused to become part of such a monstrous scheme. He threatened to publicly denounce her. Enraged by Courtenay's honesty, she stabbed him to death and then fled from the scene of her crime. The dead man's uncle then exposed her crime and the police put out a warrant for her arrest.'

'She was indeed a most wicked woman!' Trollope declared.

'That wasn't the worst of it. Throughout all her trial she showed not an ounce of repentance at what she'd done. Instead she kept pretending she was a victim of both men and refused to be tried under her married name. She continued to make out that she'd suffered at the hands of both her husband and his uncle until her own parents told the court that was a lie. I thought Mr Harding was wasting his time in seeing her. I told him an unrepentant woman wasn't worthy of God's mercy.'

'And what did he say?'

'He said that God's mercy is offered to all and that he hoped to incline her heart to seek forgiveness.'

'And so you took him to her cell?'

'Reluctantly I did. I knew he would find it painful to see a well-bred woman held in a cell for the condemned. The fifteen cells used for that purpose are not designed for comfort. Each measures just nine feet by six feet and is lit only by a small doubly grated window. When we got there Catherine Farrell was sitting in an unwashed state on a filthy bench. Her face was hidden from us because she was looking downwards at a small bundle that lay in her lap. Mr Harding looked around in dismay at the noxious damp oozing its way through the blackened brickwork and he tried in vain to block the stench of urine and excrement from his nostrils by covering his nose with his handkerchief. As he entered she glanced up at him. She didn't look the part of a murderess nor was there any hint of maliciousness in her face. All Mr Harding saw was her melancholy and hopelessness.'

'I'm not surprised. The woman must've been in despair at the fate that awaited her.'

'Yes, but that had not yet made her repentant. "I hope you've not come just to preach at me, sir," she said. "If you have, then I warn you that words alone will fall on deaf ears. Why should I regret removing William Courtenay from this world? Only I truly know the suffering he caused me and I tell you that he deserved far worse than I inflicted upon him."

'"Aren't you afraid of meeting your maker and facing his judgement?" replied Mr Harding. "Don't you fear eternal damnation more than the hangman's noose?"

'She frowned and replied in an undertone that was hardily audible, "I've already spent years living in hell so why should I turn to a God who has long abandoned me? All I ask is that you should persuade the authorities to commute my sentence to one of imprisonment or transportation. Let them show the mercy that God has not."'

'Surely she should've known that he could do nothing in that respect?'

'Even for the hopeless it's hard to give up hope of living, sir. Mr Harding told her that she should accept that murdering a person deserved the death sentence and that her sin deserved damnation unless she threw herself on God's mercy. "God's mercy! What does that mean to someone whose life has known nothing but misery?" she exclaimed. "Look at me! I'm cut off from the companionship of any friend or family member. God has never listened to my prayers so what do I know of His love?"'

Gaunt seemed to sense that Trollope was finding it hard not to pity the woman just like Mr Harding had all that time ago. Neither man had seen the evil side of human nature in the way that he had experienced it over many years. He saw their generosity of spirit as mere naivety. He pursed his lips in disapproval before continuing his account. 'Mr Harding fell silent but I reminded Catherine Farrell that life isn't fair and none should use their own misery as an excuse for crime. When she wailed, "What will happen to me?", I told her in no uncertain terms.'

'Told her what?'

'That she'd be woken in the early hours of the next day by the sound of the workmen fixing the cross-beams and uprights on the scaffold; that the bell of St Sepulchre's would ring at 7.30 to announce the hour of execution was drawing near; that she'd be led through what we call "the debtor's door" to where the mob awaited; that she and the other prisoners would be lined up on the scaffold where each would have a hanging chain attached to the hemp around their neck; and that she'd have a white cap placed over her face and have her ankles strapped together before having the noose placed round her throat.'

'Enough, enough!' interrupted Trollope, horrified

by the gaoler's catalogue of cruelty. 'I find these details of a public hanging far too shocking. Poor woman, it must have been dreadful for her to hear her forthcoming fate.'

'I meant it to shake her and it did. She asked me if it would be painful. I told her that much depended on the executioner, and that if he did his job well then her neck would be quickly broken and if he didn't she'd dangle until she slowly suffocated. At that she looked truly terrified. She turned to Mr Harding and pleaded that he should pray that the hangman knew his business. He told her he'd do as she requested but unless she repented he could do nothing to stop the terrible pain that she'd experience once she was consigned to the flames of hell. He said escape from that agony rested in her prayers and not his.

'"Then help me to pray!" she exclaimed. "Show me this day some evidence of your God's love and do not just speak of it. Only then may I have cause to repent."' Gaunt paused to wipe some spittle from his mouth with the back of his hand and then continued. 'She asked if Mr Harding had any family. He told her that he was married but had no children because of the frailty of his wife's health. She then opened up the bundle that was on her lap. I knew what lay within it but the sight came as a great shock to him. It was her child, an infant girl but a few days old. She'd asked to have it brought to her so she could hold it for the last time. Now she thrust it into his arms. I could see that his heart went out to the unsuspecting babe as one of its tiny hands appeared to clutch at the watch that dangled from his waistcoat.'

So vivid was Gaunt's account that Trollope almost felt he was there in the cell with the murderess and her child. 'Poor innocent,' he interjected as he envisaged the harrowing scene. 'The infant child had no concept that Mr Harding's timepiece was ticking away the little time left that her mother had to live.'

'But her mother knew,' said the former gaoler grimly. '"Take my baby!" Catherine Farrell begged. "Look at her! Is she not pretty? Is she not innocent? Yet when I die tomorrow morning I know she will also be condemned. Those responsible for her care will say she's a child of sin. They'll treat her with contempt and ensure she's brought up in the direst poverty in the workhouse. Promise me that you'll rescue my daughter. Promise me that you'll care for her. Show her the love that you say God has for us and I promise you that I'll immediately repent of all that I've done. I'll give nothing but praise to you and your God."'

Kind man though he was, Trollope was repelled. 'I can understand the woman's desperation, but what she asked was outrageous!'

'I was as shocked as Mr Harding when she said it. I'd not expected her to make such a last-minute plea. I told her in no uncertain terms that it was her actions that had led to the child's position and she couldn't expect any such intervention. Mr Harding's response was much the same, though he couched his reply more kindly. He told her that he was prepared to do anything in his power to bring her back to God, but what she asked was impossible. He suggested that Lord Hazleworth was a better choice to become the child's guardian.'

'A sensible thing to say.'

'Yes, but, on hearing that, Catherine Farrell cried out as if she'd been lashed with a whip. She screamed that she could never entrust her child to such a monster. She claimed that he'd have only one aim – to make her daughter suffer for her mother's crimes. She said even the workhouse would be a better place for her child than his home.'

'She must have had strong reason to hate him if she said that. We all know that workhouses are known for their barbarity.'

Gaunt agreed. 'Mr Harding had seen enough of the conditions that operate in such places to tremble at what lay ahead of the poor babe. Catherine Farrell saw the pity in his face and pressed her case more strongly. She pleaded with him, saying, "If I've to die knowing my child will suffer for my crimes then I'll have no option but to curse God. If you and your wife have no child, why not take my infant, my innocent daughter who tomorrow will be motherless as well as fatherless. Save her and in the process save also my soul." I saw in her eyes a hint of the madness that must have possessed her when she killed her unfortunate husband, but Mr Harding averted his gaze from her distraught face and chose instead to look at the child that lay in his lap.'

Trollope knew the outcome before Gaunt said anything more. How could a kind man like Mr Harding reject Catherine Farrell's plea if it meant consigning the poor child to a life of misery and its mother to damnation? 'I expect its sweet face argued far more forcibly than anything its mother could say,' he said.

The bedesman's eyes conveyed his agreement. 'I can still hear as if it was yesterday exactly what Mr Harding told her. He said in a very calm voice, "I'll care for your child as if she was mine but I'll do so for her sake and not for yours."'

'It was a courageous decision!'

'Rather say it was a foolish one! I tried to make him change his mind. I told him what he was doing was a rash act and one that he would later regret. I begged him to reconsider. "Think what you will do, sir," I said, "when this child grows to be a young woman and you see her begin increasingly to resemble her mother not only in look but also in deed. Will you not then remember what wicked acts her mother committed and fear that she may repeat them?"'

'But my guess is that you did not dissuade him from taking the child?'

'He told me that what I was saying was nonsense! He said that she would grow up surrounded by love and that would more than compensate for the example set by a mother whom she'd only known for a few hours. He took a vow, saying to the child's mother, "I'll give this child all the advantages of a loving home and I'll provide her with a fine education. Each day she'll know the blessings of having God's word read to her. Surrounded by kindness and supported by prayer, she'll walk a virtuous path throughout her life." I confess, sir, I was moved by his words, but that didn't prevent me pointing out that the child would want to know of her real mother. The knowledge of her mother's crimes would contaminate her. On hearing my words, Catherine Farrell shouted out, "Let her grow up thinking she is his daughter. There's no reason why she should be burdened with the knowledge of my criminality."'

'That was a brave thing for a mother to say,' commented Trollope, 'but surely both she and Mr Harding must have known that people would ask questions about the child's origins. A baby girl can't just appear from nowhere! And what of Mr Harding's wife? How would she react to having a murderess's child foisted upon her?'

'I said exactly that, sir, but Mr Harding said he'd no doubt that his wife would love her as if she were her own, once she saw the pretty child. He said that they could easily pass off the infant as their own because they could leave London and start a new life in some rural area far removed from the city.'

'Is that why he came to Barchester?'

'Yes, though I told him that he'd one day rue his action. I said, "This little child may look innocent enough now but one day she'll turn into a viper. The vices of parents are always inherited by their children. The girl will take after her real mother."'

'And what did he say to that?'

'He said that he'd pray that the little child should take after her father because from what he'd heard he was a good man until he came under the influence of his nephew's wife. I confess I laughed at such naivety and even Catherine Farrell looked taken aback, though she said nothing. I told Mr Harding that the child's father was also fatally flawed because he'd surrendered his judgement to an evil woman just like Adam did to Eve. I told him that, although the child looked innocent, it carried seeds of sin from both its parents. Just as a child may inherit some disease and so end up deaf or dumb or blind or crippled, so this child would inherit wickedness. I predicted the only outcome for him and his wife was one of grief.'

Trollope thought Mr Harding's action was ill advised but he did not believe the child was inevitability doomed to share the nature of its mother and father. 'You make humanity sound like a machine that is preprogrammed, Mr Gaunt,' he criticized. 'Yet we each have a soul and surely that soul is open to good influence. I believe God has the power to wash away the sinfulness of any human being.'

'You're as soft as Mr Harding, sir. That's more or less what he said.'

Such was the look on the old man's face that Trollope knew it was pointless to argue with him. Gaunt was unlikely to change a lifetime's opinion. 'So what happened next?' he asked.

'I was sent out of the cell while Catherine Farrell made her confession to Mr Harding. I don't know what she said but I've never seen a man leave a prison cell so shaken by what he'd been told. If you ask me, she probably spoke of many more crimes than had come to the knowledge of the court! Mr Harding then asked me to make arrangements for the infant to be looked after by a wet nurse until he was in a position to come and take her to a new home away from London. I did as I was bid and he paid me well for my troubles because it was many, many months before the child was collected.'

'Why was there such a delay?'

'Because, unbeknown to Mr Harding, his wife had been carrying their first child for a number of months. As you can imagine, that complicated matters. It was only when I came here after my accident and heard how Mr Harding's wife had died in childbirth that I realized what a difficult time he must've had.'

'So which one of Mr Harding's daughters is the child of Catherine Farrell?'

'That I don't know, sir. Only he can tell you that.'

'And what of Catherine Farrell?'

'She died the next day. It's not often the public gets a chance to see a woman hung so the mob was twice as large as usual. I can see her now in her black gown ascending the steps that led to the gallows. Her face was white as starched linen. The hangman told her to remove her bonnet. She stood frozen-like while he securely tied her arms to her sides, put the white cap on her head, strapped her ankles together and adjusted the rope around her neck. She muttered something about it being hard to die so young and never feel God's sunshine on her face again but she made no attempt to resist. Nor publicly did she express any remorse over what had led her to that spot. The hangman thrust a handkerchief in her hand and told her to drop it when she was ready. It seemed an eternity before she gave the signal but in reality it must've been just a minute or so. The hangman drew the bolt and did his job well. Her neck snapped quickly and her body slowly swung round and round. There she remained until the requisite hour for public display of the corpse had passed.'

Trollope could not help shuddering at the manner

of her death and an eerie silence filled the room at the completion of Gaunt's account. It was broken when the bedesman grimly concluded, 'And the same fate awaits her daughter because I'm sure she's behind the murder of Thomas Rider and Jeremiah Smith. She must have found out that they knew her secret and wanted to silence them.'

The full enormity of what John Gaunt had told him slowly began to sink into Trollope's mind. As far as all of Barchester was concerned, Eleanor and Susan Harding were the natural daughters of the warden, yet one of them was actually the illegitimate child of a convicted killer. Did the daughters know this or did they both think they were true sisters? Perhaps even more importantly, did Dr Grantly know? If it became public knowledge that the archdeacon's wife was possibly the child of Catherine Farrell it would completely destroy his ecclesiastical career. Was that enough motive for him to kill anyone who might have discovered the secret? And what of John Bold? He obviously loved Eleanor Harding. Would he kill to protect her from being shamed? Any hope of a successful medical career would be ruined if it were thought he contemplated marriage with a murderess's daughter. Then there was Mr Harding. Good man though he was, would he murder to protect the reputation of the daughters he loved? Nor could it be ruled out that either Eleanor or Susan had committed murder. A knife blow to the heart was not beyond the strength of an impassioned woman. Perhaps Gaunt was right and one of the two women had indeed inherited her mother's criminality.

6

HIDDEN IDENTITY

Anthony Trollope knew there was no way he could convey to the inspector what John Gaunt had told him without that eventually exposing the terrible story of Catherine Farrell to the public gaze. Nor was it appropriate to try and speak about it to either John Bold or Dr Grantly, who, for all he knew, might be totally in the dark about what Mr Harding had done. Indeed, he assumed that was their position, though he could not rule out that one of them knew and was prepared to kill to prevent the secret becoming known. If Gaunt was right, then at least one of Mr Harding's daughters knew the secret and was the murderer. But he had no idea which one. If it was Eleanor Harding, he had been foolish not to pass on Crumple's information to the inspector. The only viable option he had left was to speak in private to Mr Harding, but he knew even that was not without risk. There was a possibility – admittedly remote – that the warden was the killer. A loving parent will do anything to protect his child.

Obtaining an opportunity to speak with the

warden without others being present proved difficult and Trollope did not achieve it until shortly before supper. When he entered the book-lined study, Mr Harding was sitting on his accustomed chair at his desk, trying to compose a sermon for Sunday but without much success because his mind was taken up too much with the two murders. He laid down his pen and Trollope took this to mean his arrival was a welcome distraction.

'I had a long conversation with John Gaunt this afternoon,' Trollope said as he sat down opposite Mr Harding.

'And did he tell you of our long association?' Mr Harding queried, sensing his visitor's disquiet.

'Yes, and of a kind act undertaken by you many years ago.'

The warden's face visibly whitened but his manner remained calm. 'Then he has told you about Newgate?'

Trollope indicated that he had and Mr Harding looked as if the bottom had dropped out of his world. He dropped his head into his hands in the manner of someone who was about to be physically sick. Then he resorted to what he always did in moments of high stress. His hands went out to play his imaginary violincello. Trollope watched the strange movements of the warden's hands and saw in their frenzied playing the extent of the emotional storm that was sweeping through Mr Harding's mind. Unsure what to do, he could only watch and hope that the sound-less music would eventually soothe the unfortunate man before any member of his family entered and saw the havoc that his words had wrought on him. It seemed an eternity before Mr Harding's trembling hands suddenly came to an abrupt stop and the eyes that had glazed over looked at him again.

'Forgive me, Mr Trollope. I thought I had prepared myself for such a moment but I was wrong.'

'There is nothing to forgive, Mr Harding – not now nor in what happened all those years ago. You took pity on an innocent child and offered her a good home and, even more importantly, your love.'

'It's kind of you to say so, but you know as well as I that most people will not view it like that. They've not seen what I saw when I took my decision – a woman slumped on a stone seat in a damp dungeon lit just by one barred and grimy high window. A woman clutching the one thing she loved while her every muscle quivered with agony at what lay ahead of her. A woman, lost and stupefied, who would rather accept the fires of hell than seek forgiveness from a God whom she felt had deserted her. Nor have they heard what I heard. A woman begging me to fulfil my calling as a Christian minister as she clutched at any straw that might yet save her child.'

The warden's hands momentarily resumed their playing before he could continue speaking. 'I thought that I'd buried the past completely when I came here to Barchester. You can imagine what a shock it was to me when John Gaunt arrived in the city. If he spoke about what had happened then I knew neither my daughters nor I would ever be able to show our faces in public again. Fortunately he promised not to tell anyone about Catherine Farrell and I was able to arrange for the poor man to have residence at Hiram's.'

'Are you implying that he blackmailed you into giving him a position here?'

'No, that's not in his nature.'

Trollope had been deeply moved by the warden's outpouring but it did not prevent him trying to make Mr Harding focus on the present rather than the past. 'I understand your disquiet, sir, and, for that reason, I would prefer not to share with others what Gaunt told me. But there have been two deaths and it is highly probable that the murders were to prevent your secret becoming known. Mr Gaunt told Thomas Rider about Catherine Farrell and Rider conveyed the story to Jeremiah Smith. Their loose tongues were a danger. You may not like to hear it, but Mr Gaunt thinks the murderer is Catherine Farrell's child. Like it or not, you may have to tell the world which of your daughters is the cuckoo you introduced into your family nest.'

'They are both true daughters of mine in my sight. Do you think that the one who is not my flesh and blood is any less precious in my sight because of that?' Mr Harding declared vehemently. 'I've brought both of them up since they were infants. I've dandled them on my knee, wiped away their tears, read them stories at night. I've seen them both grow in beauty and in character. Would you have me destroy one in order to save the other? What kind of choice does that leave me?'

Such was the intensity with which this was said that for the first time Trollope felt he could imagine the kind warden killing someone if it was in defence of his daughters. 'Sometimes one has to make a choice between two evils, Mr Harding,' he countered. 'If your story becomes public, you may have to choose between letting the public gossip destroy the reputation of both your daughters or letting it destroy the reputation of just one of them.'

'You may be right, sir, but that is not a choice open to me, even if I were prepared to make it.'

'What do you mean?'

'I don't know which is my child and which is the child of Catherine Farrell. I never have.'

Trollope could not disguise his amazement. 'How can that be?'

'When I told my wife about my decision to adopt the murderess's child, she was very upset. She said that I was a hopeless fool to contemplate bringing the child of such a monster into our home. I tried to reassure her. I did not divulge what Catherine Farrell had told me during her confession but I told her the woman was not as black as she had been painted. That she had suffered much before resorting to murder. When that produced no change in my wife's attitude, I described how pretty the baby was and what a difference it would make for a childless couple to have a daughter to love. In reply she confided that she was already pregnant and we needed no stranger's offspring to make us parents.' Mr Harding paused and Trollope could see from the look in the warden's eyes that his mind was reliving that scene. When he resumed, his voice had become a painful whisper. 'I won't lie to you. Her news transformed my thinking on the matter. I regretted my hasty decision in agreeing to adopt Catherine Farrell's child and I agreed to break my solemn vow.'

'So what did you do?'

'I simply left the child in the care of the wet nurse that had been recommended by John Gaunt and, God forgive me, I made a new vow. I promised my wife that I'd continue to pay for the child's welfare but I'd never make it a member of our family.'

'But you did bring the child into your home!' exclaimed Trollope. 'So what made you revert back to your original vow?'

'The death of my wife in childbirth. When the doctor brought me the news that I was not only a father but also a widower, I suffered what amounted to a complete breakdown. Although I continued to fulfil my role within the parish, it was as if part of me had died. Despite all the protestations of friends, I refused to see the child that had killed my wife or even give it a name. The doctor arranged for the baby to be taken into care until the state of my mind improved. He used a woman that he knew would be kind to her. That was the state of affairs for almost three years. I'm still not sure what brought about a recovery. All I know is that it suddenly came to me that my wife's death was nothing to do with the birth of our child. I realized that it was a punishment sent by God for having broken my word to Catherine Farrell. In that instant I knew that it was my duty to love both children. I determined to leave London with both of them and make a fresh start where their history was not known. That's why I came here to

Barchester.'

'I can see how you could pass off both children as yours. No one would challenge a newly arrived widower. However, I still don't see why you don't know which of your daughters is truly yours.'

The warden smiled at Trollope's confusion. 'I knew that I might not be able to resist loving the child of my own blood more than an adopted child. To avoid that temptation I decided that I mustn't know which child was mine and which that of Catherine Farrell.'

Trollope looked at him doubtfully. 'But surely that wasn't possible?'

'On the contrary, it was easy. I'd seen neither child for three years and so all I had to do was ensure that they were brought to me in such a way as to prevent me knowing from which home they came. They were sufficiently near in age that I could not distinguish between them and I found it easy to pass them off as non-identical twin sisters.'

'And how did you achieve that?'

'I took temporary accommodation in a hotel in London where I wasn't known. Once I'd finished making arrangements for my move to Barchester, I sent a parcel with an accompanying letter to the woman looking after my daughter and a matching parcel and letter to the woman who was bringing up Catherine Farrell's daughter. Neither, of course, knew of the existence of the other. Within each parcel there was an identical set of clothes that I'd purchased. Each accompanying letter thanked the woman for her help and then stated that, although I'd long been unwell, my health had sufficiently recovered to enable me to care for my daughter. Each woman was instructed to ensure that my daughter was dressed in the clothes provided on the Monday of the following week. On that day I arranged for their collection.'

'But surely the person who collected the girls would know from which home they came?'

The warden shook his head. 'No, because I appointed two different agents for that purpose. Neither knew of the other's existence and each collected a child on the morning of the same day and brought it to my hotel. I told the hotel manager to expect the arrival of two children but made a point of not being present when either of them arrived. In that way I could not tell which agent had brought which child. By the time I arrived back at my hotel rooms all I saw was two young girls who were dressed identically and who were fortunately not that dissimilar in facial appearance to make me know which might be mine. They were playing together thanks to the encouragement of the hotel servant who'd been selected to look after them until my return. So you see I really don't know whether Eleanor or Susan is the child of Catherine Farrell.'

'But didn't they speak of their earlier homes? They must've missed those who'd cared for them for three years and whom they'd doubtless come to view as their mothers?'

'I won't deny that both of them shed tears, but from the outset I made it clear that neither were to speak of their past to me. It helped that they took comfort in each other's company. Moreover, I had the foresight not to take them straight to Barchester where others might heed them. For six months we travelled around the country, moving on to a different place every few days. In that way I diverted them and filled their minds with new experiences. A young child's memory is short. By the time I took them to Barchester they were behaving as if they'd known each other all their lives and they looked to me as a father. It was easy to pass them both off as my own.'

'Do they know of this?'

Mr Harding sighed. 'No. I've never told either of them. Why should I destroy their happiness by telling them about something that wasn't of their making and which they can't change?'

'Don't you think that a child has the right to know who are its true parents?'

'It's easy to say that but some rights are best ignored. What possible good could come of knowing that your mother might have been a murderess who killed your father? Isn't it preferable for each of them to think that they are both the daughters of a cathedral precentor?'

Trollope could see the logic behind the warden's actions but he also recognized that the murders at the almshouse threatened to shatter the façade under which Mr Harding and his daughters had lived. 'Two men have already died because of your secret,' he said with complete candour. 'Will you risk Gaunt's life by continuing to have your family live a lie?'

Once again the warden's hands involuntarily played the violincello for a few moments. The music matched the pounding of his heart and became a kind of elegy for the two dead men whom he had regarded as friends. Only when his fingers had played the final notes did he answer. 'I know I want no more men to die but nor do I want to see the happiness of my children destroyed.' He struggled to retain his composure and blushed with annoyance at his weakness. 'Have you any idea how much I now regret not acting more honestly from the outset?' The ache of his pain was palpable.

Trollope wished that he could somehow bring peace to the warden's tortured mind but he knew that it was more important that he spoke the truth. 'Gaunt is frightened. Only his love for you is preventing him speaking out. I don't think you can rely on him remaining silent for much longer. When he spoke to me he was absolutely convinced that the murderer must be the child of Catherine Farrell. You may hate me for saying it but he may be right. And, if he's wrong, then it still has to be either someone else that you love – your true daughter or John Bold or Dr Grantly – or someone that loves you enough to kill rather than see you suffer. Which of the bedesmen would you place in that category? Would Benjamin Bunce, for example, murder his friends for your sake?'

'Enough! Enough! I can stand no more of this!' Tears ran down the warden's cheeks. 'Can you imagine what it's like to live in the knowledge that at any moment the happiness of all those you love could be destroyed? Or, worse still, to fear that someone you love may have committed murder?'

'I'm sure it is like being in hell – and therefore, whatever the cost, you must be more proactive in helping uncover the murderer.'

'So what would you do if you were in my position?' asked the warden in despair.

'First, I'd bring the whole matter into the open within your family. I think it's highly likely that your link with Catherine Farrell's child will soon enter the public domain. It's better that your family should hear everything from you than that they should discover it through the press. Then I would inform the inspector. You need to keep him on your side. If he hears about Catherine Farrell from John Gaunt or me rather than from you, he'll be bound to assume you've been deliberately trying to pervert the course of justice. For the same reason I'd also tell him about Eleanor's sleepwalking and that she and Bold were seen apparently plotting together.'

'Your advice may be sensible but it is a painful choice to make and I do not know whether I have the strength to do what you suggest. Please forgive me but I can't decide on this alone. I must tell the archdeacon and seek his view on the matter because the poor man is unwittingly involved in this tragedy. There's a one in two chance that he may possibly be the husband of Catherine Farrell's daughter.'

'You realize that by telling him you may ruin your daughter's marriage? He may never forgive you for the situation in which you've placed him.'

The warden nodded and his face showed all his grief.

'And you equally realize that you can't rule out that he might be the murderer?'

'Just as you can't rule out that I'm the murderer,' Mr Harding retaliated.

'My mind acknowledges that what you say is true but my heart tells me that you're innocent.'

The warden said nothing but rang the servant's bell. When Mrs Winthrop entered, he instructed her to tell the archdeacon that his presence in the study was required as soon as was convenient. Only then did he address Trollope again. 'I would value your presence when I inform Dr Grantly about Catherine Farrell,' he said quietly. 'You've a sharp mind and there may be questions about recent events that you may be better placed to answer than I.'

Trollope immediately agreed to stay. 'I'll do all that I can to help you. Your kindness all those years ago deserves a happier outcome than this, but it's often the case that good intentions can lead to bad consequences. I learnt that as a child.'

'In what way?'

'My father was a highly educated man and a very successful barrister in London. Unfortunately he decided that he should set himself up as a country gentleman and to that end he leased farmland near Harrow. It was a big mistake. He had neither the fortune nor the expertise to succeed. As a consequence our family descended into a genteel poverty and at school I was subjected to daily ridicule by my fellow pupils, who saw I had no pocket money and not much in the way of clothes.'

'Why didn't he just return to London?'

'In his depressed state he resorted to medication and that seemed to make him increasingly unable to control his temper. As a consequence he lost all his clients.'

'It must've been very difficult for you and the rest of your family.'

'Yes, but worse was to come. My parents moved to America to create a new life there and I was sent to Winchester College as a boarder. However, my college bills weren't paid and the school tradesmen were told not to extend any credit to me. The teachers despised me and regularly flogged me. I had no friend to whom I could pour out my sorrows. Such was my plight that one day I contemplated ending my life by jumping off the top of the college tower. I was rescued from suicide only by my father's return. He rented a farmhouse and sent me as a day boy to Harrow, but my fate there was no better. What right had a wretched farmer's boy, reeking from the dunghill, to sit next to the sons of peers, or, even worse, the sons of rich tradesmen who were paying thousands of pounds to board their sons there? The indignities I endured are not to be described.'

What further account might have followed this was interrupted by the arrival of Dr Grantly. Mr Harding greeted him with obvious apprehension and then stated, 'I've summoned you here to confess that I've done you a great wrong. Mr Trollope is here because he knows the circumstances and may be able to answer some questions that I can't. '

Dr Grantly heard with mounting horror what Trollope had to say. It was obvious from his manner that he had possessed no prior knowledge of the warden's deception and that it came as a huge shock to him that he might be married to the child of a woman who had been publicly hung for her crimes. After

hanged

asking Trollope a few questions to clarify exactly the extent of John Gaunt's knowledge of the situation, he suddenly gave vent to his anger at what his father-in-law had done. 'How could you do this? What folly possessed you!' he stormed.

The warden began playing his imaginary violincello as if his life depended on it and his eyes took on such a haunted look that Trollope feared for the poor man's sanity.

"Twas enough kindness to pay for a woman to bring up the child without bringing her into your home!' continued Dr Grantly. 'Your dead wife must be turning in her grave at what you've done. Not only have you made your daughter grow up alongside this monstrous woman's child but you've pretended they're of equal worth!'

Mr Harding's hand paused mid stroke and suddenly a look of defiance replaced the anguish. 'I should not have to remind you that all are of equal worth in the sight of God,' he said, 'and both Susan and Eleanor are of equal worth in mine!'

'Damn it, sir, this is no time to preach at me!' retaliated the archdeacon and he vented his anger by sweeping his right hand across the warden's desk, scattering the precious musical manuscripts that lay on its surface to the floor. Trollope decided that either Dr Grantly was a superb actor or the story of Mr Harding's secret had come as a genuine and devastating blow. If it was the latter then it was very likely that he had no hand in the murders. He would have had no reason to do so.

'I might not have loved them equally had I not

taken the action I did,' continued the warden. 'And would Susan and Eleanor have developed the same kind of loving relationship that they did? I doubt it. And think of the child itself. How would knowing her mother murdered her father have helped Catherine Farrell's child grow up with a balanced mind? What I did may have been wrong, but, until today, it brought peace and happiness. It made Susan and Eleanor the people they are, the daughters I love, and, dare I say it, in Susan's case, the woman you courted and married.'

'Possibly to my cost!' replied the archdeacon. 'This will seriously jeopardize my chance of becoming a bishop.' The tone and manner in which this was said made Trollope fear that their news might have shattered once and for all the happiness of the marriage. However, both of them had underestimated Dr Grantly's deep affection for his wife and the high regard in which he held her. The archdeacon paused and wiped his face with his hands as if somehow that would restore his equanimity. Then he looked up and said in a much quieter and far more controlled voice, 'Forgive me, gentlemen. I shouldn't have said that. I love my wife and nothing will make me regret for a moment marrying her. Susan has been an exemplary wife and a most loving mother to my children. If she's Catherine Farrell's child she carries no trace of her mother within her nature. Nor does Eleanor. If the world finds out about all this I'll stand by both of them and defy anyone who dares malign them!'

The warden's eyes brimmed with tears. 'Bless you!' he cried, and, to hide his emotions, he began picking up the manuscripts from the floor and returning them to his desk. Only when this was done did he ask, 'Do you think we should tell Susan and Eleanor?'

'Susan and I both made a vow when we married that we would always be truthful to each other. I'd find it difficult to keep this from her and, if she is told, I think she'll want Eleanor to also know.'

'I think it would be foolish not to tell them,' commented Trollope. 'They need to be prepared because there is every likelihood that the truth is going to enter the public arena sooner or later. Would it help if I told them? I lack your emotional involvement and so may be able to tell them more easily and in ways that might alleviate their distress.'

'That's a very kind offer, Mr Trollope, but this is a family matter and they should be told by one of us.'

'And it should be me who does it,' interrupted the warden, 'because I'm responsible for all of this. I'll go at once to their rooms. Pray for me, gentlemen, that I may find the right words.' He moved to the door, opened it, and then, before leaving, added, 'And pray for them.'

No sooner had he gone than Dr Grantly turned to Trollope and declared bluntly, 'This is a terrible business. Few men would have so foolishly promised to bring up the child of such an evil woman. My father-in-law is often too kind and generous in his dealings with people. I don't wish to sound melodramatic but I fear he'll not cope with what he has to face over the coming days and that his mental health will suffer as a consequence unless somehow you and I protect him.'

'I'm willing to assist in whatever way I can, but I

fail to see what I can do.'

'You can go back to London and see if you can uncover which of his daughters is the child of Catherine Farrell. Why should both suffer? If it's my wife, I'll seek another position in the Church to take her away from the scandal. If necessary, we'll leave the country together and undertake mission work. If it's Eleanor, then I'll arrange for her to work as a governess in France, where she can hopefully build a new life for herself. I would undertake the investigation myself but I daren't leave my father-in-law here unsupported.'

'I will do as you ask, but it'll not be easy after all these years to ascertain the truth. At the time Mr Harding did all he could to cover his tracks.'

'See if you can trace those who brought the children to him in London. Better still, trace those who cared for the two girls. I refuse to believe that there's not someone somewhere who can give us a clue to their true identities.'

'I'll do what I can but I think it would help if I had the assistance of Inspector Blake.'

'What?! Tell that nincompoop! He'll blab the tale around the town before the day is out!' exclaimed the archdeacon.

'You will all be placed in a terrible situation if you don't tell him and he finds out for himself. As I said earlier, he'll think that you've deliberately tried to pervert the cause of justice and he may communicate that to the press.'

'Damn it, you may be right!'

Their conversation was interrupted by the

unexpectedly early return of the warden. His face was ashen white. 'I went to tell Susan first but she already knew!' he gasped.

'How? And why has she said nothing to you or me about it?' responded Dr Grantly, looking like a man whose world had suddenly fallen apart.

7

FAMILY RESPONSES

MRS GRANTLY SWEPT into the room close after her father before he could say any more. Her face looked flushed and Trollope could see small beads of perspiration on her forehead. She eyed the three men nervously and then hurriedly moved across to her husband. 'Pray forgive me for keeping this matter secret,' she pleaded as she grasped hold of his hands. 'I know I should have had the courage to tell you about the mystery surrounding my birth, but I feared to risk our happiness by telling you. Although my heart told me that you wouldn't let anything come between us, my head gave me a hundred reasons why you should cast me aside.'

'How could you possibly think that?'

'Not because I doubted your character but because I know what others would begin to say if they found out. Their malice would not be content with shaming my father. Nor would it be satisfied with encouraging people to avoid Eleanor and me on the grounds that one of us was almost certainly the spawn of the devil. They would also wish to bring you down. They would say that in marrying me you had shown a severe lack of judgement and helped introduce a monstrous cuckoo into the cathedral nest. Those who currently see you as the natural successor to your father as Bishop of Barchester would turn against you. How could you not resent me for that? Overnight my ancestry would have negated all those years in which you've worked tirelessly to promote the interests of the Church.'

Dr Grantly sought to reassure her. 'You should have listened to your heart rather than your head, Susan. I will not deny that I would like to follow in my father's footsteps and I believe that I've the qualities to make a good bishop, but you matter far more to me than any ambition.' His wife bit her lip and tried in vain to disguise her emotion. The atmosphere in the small study seemed to crackle with the intensity of the moment. The archdeacon then voiced the question that all three men in the room wanted answered, 'How long have you known?'

'I only discovered the truth when Papa moved here to become the warden and vacated the home in which we'd all lived for so many years. If I'd known about Catherine Farrell when you asked me to marry you, I would never have consented to become your wife because I would rather have remained a spinster then place your career in jeopardy.'

Dr Grantly sighed. 'You have removed a great weight from my shoulders because I'd begun to fear that you might have been deceiving me for years.'

She turned her head towards her father. 'If you

recall, Papa, I decided that you ought to get rid of much of what you had accumulated over the years before you moved. In that process I took it upon myself to sort through two large boxes that contained lots of old paperwork in order to burn everything that was obviously not worth keeping. Within one of the boxes I found a small bundle of old letters. They were letters from the man who had been Papa's doctor in London before he came to work here in Barchester.'

'I was a wretched fool not to have disposed of those years ago.'

'Don't worry. They no longer exist. Once I'd read them I showed them only to Eleanor and then we agreed to destroy them. We didn't want any other person to see what they contained.'

'So Eleanor knows too!' groaned Mr Harding, involuntarily striking chords on his imaginary violin-cello in his distress. 'Why did neither of you talk to me about it?'

'We'd no desire to upset you, Papa. Why should we force you to speak of this matter when you'd gone to such great lengths to hide the truth from us?'

Conflicting emotions swept across Trollope's mind as he observed the drama unfolding before him. He admired Dr Grantly's fortitude and forgiveness and was amazed by the strength of character shown by Mr Harding's two daughters. Few women would not have sought greater clarification on such a matter of personal importance. However, he was horrified to hear of Mrs Grantly's awareness of Catherine Farrell and the danger she posed. It made her – and, of course, Eleanor Harding – the prime suspects in the investigation. What would the inspector do, especially if he relayed what Jonathan Crumple had told him about Eleanor Harding's movements prior to both murders? 'Your tactfulness does you both credit, Mrs Grantly,' he said, trying to disguise his alarm, 'but would you mind telling us exactly the extent of the information that you uncovered in those letters?'

Mrs Grantly turned towards him. It was almost as if she had noticed his presence in the room for the first time. Her face turned pink with the blood that rushed to her cheeks. 'We learnt that Eleanor and I could not be sisters,' she said, her voice tense and low. 'The first letter that I opened was a letter of condolence from the doctor who had attended Mama in childbirth. It was quite clear from its contents that she had given birth to her first and only child. Can you imagine what I felt when I read that? All the certainties in my life instantly disintegrated.' She paused and for a brief moment looked on the verge of tears, but was able to recover and resume. 'I learnt from the doctor's subsequent letters how increasingly depressed Papa had become in the wake of his wife's death and how the child was eventually sent away into care.'

'And how did you discover the existence of Catherine Farrell?'

'Other correspondence referred to payments also being made for the upkeep of an entirely different infant girl. I was unsure where this child had come from until I read the last letter in the bundle I'd found. In it Papa's doctor offered various reasons as to why Papa shouldn't execute his plan to bring both girls up as his natural daughters. That included some very derogatory comments about the other child's origin. It was in those passages that I read how Papa had vowed to bring up the daughter of the murderess prior to her execution.'

'That must also have come as a terrible shock,' commented Trollope sympathetically.

'Yes, it did. At first I thought I would tell no one of what I'd discovered, not even Eleanor, but she detected my unhappiness and she wouldn't rest until I'd confided in her the cause of my grief.'

'And what was her response?'

'She was equally upset but she said it made sense of memories we had both suppressed. People never entirely forget their past and we had long been puzzled why each of us appeared to have vague recollections of people and places that were unknown to the other and unconnected to Barchester.'

'I find it amazing that both of you were able to keep this discovery to yourselves,' interposed Dr Grantly.

'Eleanor and I saw no reason to upset anyone. We agreed the letters were a thing of the past and best destroyed and forgotten. Neither of us could have wished for a more loving father or for a more loving sister. We have grown up together and been such constant companions that no blood relations could be closer. What Catherine Farrell did and what happened to her means nothing to either of us. She gave up her rights to call one of us daughter twenty years ago! She was never part of our lives.' These last sentences were said with not only vehemence but also a hint of defiance.

'I agree, my child, I agree!' sobbed the warden.

'And so do I,' added her husband, 'but sadly the world may not. Is not that the case, Mr Trollope?'

'I fear so.'

'I'm not naïve. As I have already said, I'm all too aware of what some of the ladies of Barchester would say,' replied Mrs Grantly sharply. 'That's why I decided to have the letters destroyed. So there would be no evidence.'

'Unfortunately there is every reason to believe that the two bedesmen were killed to stop them speaking about your family's secret,' pointed out Trollope. 'That leaves not only your father but also you and your sister as the prime suspects.'

'You can't be serious! Anyone who knows us would find the idea of any of us committing murder laughable!' she exclaimed.

'It's a pity you and your sister ever read that correspondence because ignorance was your best chance of proving your innocence. The only way now is to find someone else who would want the story suppressed.'

Mrs Grantly's eyes widened with horror. 'But who but us would desire that?' she asked shakily.

'Your father is deeply loved by many of the bedesmen. It's possible that one of them has acted to protect him.' He saw hope return to her eyes and took pleasure in it before providing her with less happy news. 'I've advised Mr Harding that he should inform the inspector of all that we know so that he can hopefully identify the killer.'

'I don't think Mr Blake can be trusted to keep our secret,' she replied witheringly. 'I don't want him told.'

'Mr Trollope thinks that would not be wise,' interjected her husband. 'It could put us all in a bad light if the story leaks out and it becomes known that we kept him in the dark about it.'

'Mrs Grantly bristled like a stuck pig and said in a voice that brooked no contradiction, 'I would prefer to take that risk. For all we know the murders may have another cause and we will have wrecked our reputation for nothing.'

'I agree,' commented her father.

Dr Grantly saw the determination in his wife's face and chose not to argue. 'Then the matter is closed,' he announced.

Trollope said nothing but he felt deeply frustrated. It was plain to him that the family was acting like an ostrich burying its head in the sand. Two men had been murdered and what other cause could there possibly be for their deaths? The inspector was not going to just abandon his investigation. Sooner or later John Gaunt would reveal what he knew – unless, of course, he was also murdered. Dare he therefore respect the family's wishes and risk that man's life? Or should he tell the police what he had been told in confidence? Mrs Grantly was a resourceful woman and one who would do anything she could to protect her husband and children from scandal. Had she refused to let them tell the inspector because she was the murderer?

Mrs Grantly looked relieved and gave first her husband and then her father an affectionate kiss. 'Papa, we must speak with Eleanor,' she said, 'so that she is equally circumspect on this matter. Will you accompany me to her room?' This question was said in such a way that it again left no room for disagreement.

Hardly had they left the study than Dr Grantly dejectedly sank into a chair. He looked anxiously at Trollope and muttered, 'I cannot go against their wishes but I agree with you. We'll not be able to keep the matter of Catherine Farrell secret and then our silence will have made matters worse.' There was not a trace in his face of the composure that he had shown in his wife's presence. 'Mr Trollope, I beg that you will help me.'

'In what way?'

'Go back to London. Do whatever you can to find the evidence that will prove my wife is not Catherine Farrell's child. I know her. She's not capable of having committed these crimes. Nor is Mr Harding. Though it pains me to say it, I believe that Eleanor must have committed the murders. I think you will find that it is she who carries tainted blood within her veins.'

'And what if I find that it's your wife who is Catherine Farrell's child?'

'You won't. My wife is an angel. There's not an ounce of bad blood in her. Eleanor is a good enough girl but she has weaknesses – not least her interest in that young and dangerous doctor, Mr Bold. I would not be surprised if the pair of them are behind the murders!'

'But you've no evidence that Eleanor has told John Bold about Catherine Farrell,' protested Trollope.

'Then look into that also. If I were a gambling man, I would bet everything I have that she's told him.'

Trollope was unhappy at the evident bias in the

archdeacon's mind, but he registered that it was natural for a husband to defend his wife's position. He also knew that it made sense for the family to try and discover the truth. After a momentary reflection he said, 'I'll go back to London as soon as the inspector permits that and I'll do what I can, but only on two conditions.'

'What are they?'

'First, that I should speak with Eleanor about Catherine Farrell.'

'What good would that do?'

'It might clarify whether she has told Mr Bold. It's also possible that she knows more than your wife and she may provide some clue that I can follow.'

'She is more likely to mislead you, but I assent to your condition.'

'Good. And my second condition is that, if I discover your wife is Catherine Farrell's child, you'll not expect me to stay silent on the matter to the other members of your family.'

The archdeacon shrugged his shoulders. 'I assent to that also because I'm sure that will not be the outcome of your investigations.'

The two men shook hands and shortly afterwards Trollope decided to return to his room to rest. Scarce had he arrived within it than there was a gentle knock on his door. He opened it and outside in the corridor stood Mrs Grantly. Her eyes flashed angrily at him. 'I'm sorry to disturb you, Mr Trollope,' she stated, 'but I must see you and in private.'

'Please come in.'

She entered the room with a look of deep

determination. 'What I've to say will not take long,' she said and the coldness in her voice was chilling. 'In my opinion it's most unfortunate that you've become a party to our family secret. I will therefore be blunt. I don't want you poking your nose any further into our affairs and I want you to cease offering advice to my father and husband.'

'Not even if I could help find out whether you or your sister is the child of Catherine Farrell?'

'I've already said I've no interest in knowing the truth on that topic. As far as I'm concerned I'm the daughter of Mr Harding and I'm Eleanor's sister. The issue of whether the same blood flows in my veins means absolutely nothing to me.' She jabbed at him with her right forefinger. 'I want you to keep out of this matter altogether and I want your solemn word that you'll say nothing to anyone about my family's connection to Catherine Farrell.'

'I'm sorry, Mrs Grantly, but I'll not give you what you ask,' he replied. 'I can promise that I'll not lightly reveal your family's secret, but too much has happened here for me to guarantee never to speak about it. Two men have been murdered.'

'Their deaths may not be connected with this.'

'But they most probably are. I'll let the inspector undertake his investigation and if, at some point, I judge I must tell him, then I will.'

'I beg you to reconsider, Mr Trollope. You could destroy this family in the process! I ask not for myself but because the resulting outcry will destroy my husband's career, wreck any chance Eleanor has for happiness, and more than likely kill my father.

Think also of the impact that it will have on my step-children. Their lives too will be blighted. Think what their schoolmates will say to them if they think their grandmother was a murderess!'

'I'm sorry, Mrs Grantly. I sympathize with your position but I can't give you the promise you seek.'

'You show the strangest sympathy, sir, when you decline to offer the one thing that would put my mind at rest! You told me that you would one day like to be a successful novelist. That will never happen if you lack the imagination to see how this information could destroy us!'

'I've no doubt that your lives would become intolerable, but I believe that sometimes telling the truth is more important than anything else. What I will promise is that I'll not tell the inspector what I know without first informing your father and husband that I intend to do so.'

Mrs Grantly stiffened. For a moment he thought that she was going to strike him. However, she recovered herself and then said in a menacing tone, 'I'm not without influence, sir. If you betray our secret I'll see that you suffer for it! Have no doubt about that!'

'Are you threatening me, Mrs Grantly?'

'I won't let you betray us!'

'You heard my answer,' he continued in as calm a voice as he could muster. 'I think you should leave.'

Fury swept across her face and, in that instant, Trollope thought he could see her killing the two bedesmen. All the kindness in her demeanour had vanished. Here was a woman who would be prepared to do anything to defend her family's reputation. She swept out of the room, slamming the door behind her. Trollope sat down in his chair and heaved a deep sigh. Had he said the right thing? If she was an innocent woman, she had deserved better treatment from him. If he put himself in her shoes, everything she had said was true. The story of Catherine Farrell would destroy not just her life but also the lives of everyone she loved. And for what purpose? Who would gain by knowing of Mr Harding's misguided act of kindness all those years ago?

His reverie was broken by an angry knock at his door. Even as he opened it, Eleanor Harding pushed her way in. 'What have you done to so upset my sister?' she demanded.

Trollope briefly explained the gist of what had transpired between him and Mrs Grantly.

'I swear to you, Mr Trollope, that none of us are guilty. Someone else has committed these murders.'

'But who else has an interest in silencing the bedesmen?'

All colour left Eleanor Harding's cheeks and for a moment he thought she was going to faint. He grasped hold of her arm and gently escorted her to a chair. She sat down, trembling and wringing her hands. Trollope had the intuition to know the cause. 'Mr Bold also knows, doesn't he?' he whispered gently.

'My sister is a strong and determined woman, Mr Trollope. When she found those terrible letters she simply dismissed what they contained as being of no relevance to us. She said our lives had moved on and been blessed by God. She told me that I should never speak to Father about what she'd discovered. There was no need to revisit the past and reopen old wounds. She ordered me to speak to no one about Catherine Farrell.'

'And did you obey her?'

'No, I lacked her courage. I couldn't help worrying about what would happen if others discovered our secret. I'd no one to turn to – not Susan, not my father, not my brother-in-law.'

'And so you talked to John Bold?'

'Yes, I confided in him. He's been a loyal friend of this family since we were children together.'

'And what did he say?'

'He told me not to worry because he would never let anyone harm me.' All Eleanor's efforts to control her emotions were instantly lost as she said these words. She slumped in the seat, her head dropped into her hands and she sobbed bitterly, her shoulders heaving with her grief.

'And now you fear he may have killed the bedesmen to protect you?'

There was no answer but the failure to deny it was sufficient in itself. He waited, permitting her to gradually regain control of herself. She eventually looked up at him. Never had he seen such anguish in a person's face. 'God forgive me but I fear that he might, and I hate myself for thinking it.'

'Because you love him?'

She gave no immediate answer, but he knew that she did. 'Have you told your sister that Mr Bold knows?'

'No.'

'Then I suggest that you do not.' She looked up at him, clearly surprised by his comment, and so he explained his response. 'Let me first see if I can find some evidence to prove his innocence. If you tell your sister she will tell Dr Grantly and, knowing his dislike of Mr Bold, he will probably tell the inspector that the doctor is the murderer. You wouldn't want that to happen, would you?'

'No, but is this what we will all be reduced to? Deceiving each other about what we think and what we have done? I fear, Mr Trollope, that unless these murders are resolved soon our family will be destroyed from within. How long will it be before we can't look at each other without asking whether we are seeing the murderer?'

'You are right, Miss Harding. That's why we must find out the person responsible. I know that I upset your sister earlier and I'm sorry for that, but I promise you that I'll do whatever I can to help solve the murders and, hopefully, without the world having to know their cause. I only wish that you and your sister hadn't destroyed those letters.'

'Why?'

'For all we know there may be a clue in the past that will explain what has happened here,' Trollope explained. 'We should be investigating everything we can, including what happened all those years ago.'

'The letters are not destroyed, Mr Trollope. My sister gave them to me to read and then told me to burn them. However, I couldn't bring myself to destroy the only clues that we had to our possible true identities, even though I feared what the world might say if the letters became public knowledge. I know this may sound strange but I want to know which of us is Catherine Farrell's daughter.'

'And if it was you?'

'I think that would be a better outcome than if it turned out she was the mother of Susan. My sister is a strong woman but she would find it very hard to come to terms with having a murderess as her mother. I don't have the same problem. I don't wish to be her daughter but I would not hate being so. Catherine Farrell loved her child, Mr Trollope, and if I'm that child she deserves my love, whatever crimes she committed.'

Trollope was almost overwhelmed by her fortitude and grace. Surely a woman of her quality could not possibly be the murderer? But then his doubt resurfaced. Outwardly Catherine Farrell had appeared to be an angel. Was the same true about Eleanor Harding?

'I gave the letters to Mr Bold and begged him to help me uncover the truth,' she continued. 'He was the only person I could trust.'

Trollope could see that she did not realize her words were condemning Bold to become a strong suspect in the investigation. A young man might well kill to protect the reputation of the woman he loved. 'And did he discover anything?' he asked, choosing not to disillusion her at that moment.

'He went to London to follow up what few clues were contained within the letters. When he returned he told me that he'd been unable to find anything helpful.'

'And where are the letters now?'

'He still has them.'

'Then have I your permission to speak with him and obtain them from him?'

Eleanor Harding looked distinctly uncomfortable but nevertheless gave her assent.

8

A WIFE WRONGED

A LARGE BRASS plate engraved 'John Bold, Surgeon' on the door of Pakenham Villas informed Anthony Trollope that he had reached the right house. He paused before knocking. Poor Eleanor Harding might not have plighted her troth to this man, and perhaps she had not yet fully acknowledged how much she loved him, but Trollope had no doubt that she did. And why should she not? Her father had opened his home to him and he was young and handsome and appeared good natured and conscientious. It was true that he as yet lacked the income to support a wife, but Trollope suspected it was only a matter of time before Bold would establish himself as a doctor in Barchester, despite the opposition he faced from vested interests.

The woman who opened the door was not beautiful but nor was she unattractive and Trollope judged her to be about thirty years old. Her facial features were sufficiently alike to John Bold that he had no doubts as to her identity. 'I assume I've the pleasure of addressing Miss Bold,' he said whilst undertaking a slight bow of his head.

'I am Mary Bold, sir, but you hold the advantage because I've no idea of your identity.'

Trollope explained who he was and how he had come on behalf of Miss Harding to discuss some important business with her brother.

'I'm sorry but my brother is currently not here,' she replied. 'He's been called out to a patient. However, I'm expecting him back shortly so you're welcome to wait for him in our sitting room.'

To this Trollope willingly assented and she led him down a modest hallway into a room that was comfortably furnished though old-fashioned in its appearance. It bore signs of a family that had seen better days. His eye was mainly drawn to the many books that partially lined its walls. Trollope glanced at the shelves. Many were medical texts but there was also a smattering of historical works and books by famous novelists of the day. Mary invited him to sit on a chair and then left him to prepare a cup of tea. In her absence he was very conscious of the slow ticking of the clock on the mantelpiece. It seemed a long time but in fact it was but a few minutes before she returned with a tray laden with tea and slices of cake. Although she appeared to lack her brother's liveliness of manner, Trollope could not help but note her kind face as she began to pour him his drink. He suspected Mary Bold's faults were fewer than her virtues.

'This is very kind of you, Miss Bold,' he said, sipping his tea. 'Have you lived long here in Barchester?'

'John and I were first brought here when we were children and we both immediately fell in love with the place. The only sadness is that as yet the city has not truly welcomed my brother.'

'And why is that? He has an air of authority and his manner strikes me as being one that would put patients at their ease. '

'In part it stems from the whispering malice of the other doctors in Barchester. They know my brother has more understanding of modern medicine than they have and they are afraid that they will lose their wealthy patients. As a consequence they spread rumours that he is inexperienced and prone to experiment with untried medicines. But John doesn't help his cause. He's too outspoken about the things in Barchester that require changing.'

'He certainly seems to have upset Dr Grantly, who has not a good word to say about him. I think he regards your brother as a dangerous revolutionary.'

Mary Bold laughed. 'Nothing could be further from the truth. John wants to end any injustice that he sees but I can assure you that he's no radical. He's far too kind a man to desire any revolution.'

'That is what Miss Harding also says.'

'I count Eleanor as a friend and wish she could be more.' Mary paused and a blush spread across her cheeks. It made her appear more attractive. 'Forgive me, sir, I presume to say too much.'

Trollope smiled. 'My dear Miss Bold, it takes but a few minutes in Miss Harding's presence to see that there's a growing bond between her and your brother. And I am sure it would flourish more were Dr Grantly not so opposed to your brother being seen anywhere near the warden's house.'

The arrival of John Bold abruptly terminated their conversation. He greeted his sister with natural affection and then shook Trollope's hand warmly. His manner was open and friendly. 'Delighted to see you, sir. To what do I owe this pleasure? I hope there's no more trouble at the hospital?'

'Not at present but I fear there may be more unless the person responsible for two murders is found. For that reason, Mr Bold, I desire a word with you in private.'

'I'll leave you two men to discuss whatever you think necessary,' interjected Mary Bold graciously and she immediately left the study.

Once she had gone, Trollope explained to Bold what Eleanor Harding had told him and how he had promised to try and discover the truth about her ancestry. The doctor listened without interruption and then moved across to a desk. Taking out a key from his pocket, he unlocked one of its drawers and withdrew a bulky envelope, which he proceeded to hand over to Trollope. 'This contains the letters,' he said, 'and I wish they'd never been written for they've done nothing but awaken questions that are better left unanswered.'

Trollope glanced at what the envelope contained but resisted the temptation to instantly read the letters within it. Instead he asked, 'Did your perusal of these provide you with any clues to follow?'

Bold sat down on the chair opposite to him. Trollope could see the anxiety in his eyes as he debated within his mind how to answer. 'I'll be honest with you, sir,' he finally replied. 'Two of the letters did provide something because they each contained a reference to Catherine Farrell possessing a brother. In the first of them the doctor questioned Mr Harding's judgement in not seeking out the child's uncle.'

'And why did Mr Harding not do that?'

'That's answered in the subsequent letter. Mr Harding apparently judged the brother to be unfit to care for the child because he'd failed to support his sister during her trial and imprisonment.'

'That's a not unreasonable assumption.'

'Agreed,' said Bold, nodding, 'but it was a belief that I thought worth testing. I determined to see if I could find this brother, despite the passage of so many years. The doctor's letters gave no indication of where he might be found. All it provided was his name – Richard. Armed with that, I visited Newgate and made some enquiries, but elicited no information on the man's current whereabouts. I next went to the offices of some of the leading newspapers and asked to see copies of the articles that had appeared on the trial and execution of Catherine Farrell all those years ago. They gave a lurid picture of her crimes but they made no reference to her having any brother. At that point I almost gave up. Then I decided to take a gamble. I paid for an advertisement to go into the *Jupiter.*' Bold paused and, getting up, delved again into the drawer in his desk. This time he pulled out a page torn from a newspaper and passed it to Trollope. 'Read it for yourself.'

Trollope saw that a circle had been drawn around the relevant advertisement. It was short but to the point. In large bold print was the name 'Richard

Farrell'. Below that were two short sentences, which stated, 'Please will you contact Mr J. Bold, surgeon. He has a matter of great import to discuss with you about your sister.' Then were details of a hotel address in London.

'You'll see I took the precaution of not mentioning Barchester. For all I knew Richard Farrell was a criminal. The last thing I wanted was to give any clue that might lead him to this place.'

'And was there a response?'

'No. I waited a few days and then returned to Barchester. I told Eleanor – Miss Harding – that I'd been unable to discover anything.'

'Then I must take up the search,' Trollope said, rising to his feet.

'That will be unnecessary,' said Bold firmly.

'I don't understand.'

'About a week after I'd reported my lack of success, the hotel in London forwarded me a letter in a handwriting I did not recognize. You can imagine my excitement when I opened it and found it was from Richard Farrell. It asked me to pardon his delay in replying to the advertisement. He had been unsure whether to respond or not. Time had served to increase his curiosity and so he now requested a meeting. Because his health was frail he asked me to come to his home. The letter provided me with his address.'

'But you said nothing of this to Miss Harding?'

'No. I feared to rekindle Miss Harding's hopes. In fact I contemplated simply burning the letter. However, my own curiosity eventually led me to return to London to see him.'

'Was that not dangerous?' asked Trollope, frowning.

A look of amusement flashed across Bold's face. 'I think not. His house was in a very respectable area.'

'But that does not necessarily indicate that those who live there are respectable.'

'Agreed, but the brother's letter was signed "the Reverend Richard Farrell". I think you will agree that visiting a clergyman is not usually deemed a dangerous activity!'

For a moment Trollope was rendered speechless by this totally unexpected revelation. Then he laughed. 'So why have you told neither the warden or Miss Harding about him?' he asked, his interest truly aroused.

'For reasons that I'll make clear in a moment. But first let me tell you about Richard Farrell. I can assure you that he is a delightful man, though much worn down by the hard life that he's lived. He's physically very frail. Most of his ministry was spent undertaking missionary work in Africa. Indeed, he was working in Kuruman, a missionary outpost in South Africa, at the time of his sister's trial. Unbeknown to him, mistaken reports of his death from a severe bout of malaria had circulated in London. That's why his sister made no attempt to contact him or seek his help to look after her child. By the time the newspaper accounts of her trial and execution reached him, she had been dead several months. He came back to England at once but there was nothing he could do except mourn.'

'But surely he would have sought to find her child!'

Bold's eyes flickered. 'He was told the child had died.'

'By whom?'

'John Gaunt.'

Trollope was nonplussed. 'But why should the gaoler have lied to him?'

'I've no idea but he did and, if I'm honest, I don't much care to know why. I now regret even going to see Farrell. The last thing we want is him seeking to find his niece and stirring up the whole story of Mr Harding's actions.'

'So what reason did you give him for your advertisement?'

'I pretended that I was a nephew of the doctor who attended the birth of Catherine Farrell's baby. I told him that my uncle had recently died and in reading through his papers I had discovered that he did not believe the convicted murderess was anything like the evil monster portrayed by the press. I said that I was considering writing an article about her case, but I required firmer evidence before I could do so. Hence my advertisement. I felt he, more than anyone, would know what Catherine Farrell was truly like and would welcome a chance of having her evil reputation diminished.'

'You've a resourceful imagination, Mr Bold! And what was his response?'

'He was immensely grateful. He said that the reason for his sister's crime was much misunderstood and he proceeded to tell me about her upbringing and the events that had led to her unfortunate marriage.'

'And his account was very different from what we have been told about her?'

'Completely different,' replied Bold gravely.

'According to him, he and Catherine were made to attend church from an early age, not because of any religious conviction on the part of their parents but rather because it was deemed socially important. His father encouraged him to become a clergyman in the expectation that he would rise to become a bishop and so enable the family to mix with high society. He went to study at Oxford but after completing his studies he declined to take up the very profitable parish that was offered to him. Instead he opted to undertake missionary work abroad. You can imagine the furore that created. His parents described his religious conviction as unworldly nonsense and virtually disowned him. Their anger had unfortunate consequences for Catherine, who was ten younger than him and still little more than a girl.'

'I fail to see the connection.'

'It was quite simple. If their son was not going to bring them the wealth and position they desired, then that task had to fall to their daughter. According to Richard Farrell, they deliberately did everything they could from that moment on to turn her into a coquette. All that mattered was to make her a rich man's wife. She was brought up to believe that there was nothing as important as appearance. Clothes, however fine, were mere rags unless they were the latest fashion. Music, however beautiful, was mere noise unless it was a song sung to attract a man or a piano played to make her appear a desirable wife. Conversation had only one purpose – to make men want her – and its content was judged by its wit and not by its truthfulness. Her parents did all they could to make her cold and calculating.'

Trollope recalled his conversation with John Gaunt and the former gaoler's description of her as a woman with an angel's face and a devil's heart. He voiced his thoughts almost without realizing. 'Then they succeeded.'

'Not according to Richard Farrell. Despite all her parents' efforts to indoctrinate her into looking only for a profitable husband, Catherine fell in love with a young man who had no fortune. All he possessed was a handsome figure, a kind heart and a modest income. The latter would've been sufficient for him and Catherine to live happily and comfortably but, when he proposed and Catherine accepted, her parents vehemently refused their permission. They said such harsh things to the young man that any hopes of immediate marriage were crushed and, in his despair, the unfortunate suitor decided to seek his fortune in America in the hope he might make himself rich and so prove his worth. Catherine promised that she would marry no one else and her furious parents locked her in her room. They told everyone that she was ill and permitted no one to see her. This went on for some weeks yet Catherine remained faithful to her chosen love despite all the pressures placed on her. Then came a fateful day when her parents took delight in showing her a newspaper article. The ship on which her lover had embarked had sunk and all on board were presumed dead.'

'How tragic!'

'Yes, and at that moment Catherine cared no more what might happen to her. She wrote to her brother about all that happened and told him she'd agreed to marry whomever her parents wanted. It was they who selected William Courtenay, knowing that he was likely to inherit vast lands and a title from his uncle, Lord Hazleworth. Courtenay was easily seduced by Catherine's beauty but it was an ill day when she married him.'

'Not as ill a day as it was for him. After all, she drove him into debauchery, bankrupted him and then seduced his uncle before murdering him.'

'No, that's only the version given to and accepted by the court. According to Richard Farrell, it was far from the truth. Until she thought him dead, Catherine wrote to him about her terrible marriage. Unfortunately her letters didn't reach him until it was far too late for him to do anything.'

'So what's his version of events?'

'He told me that Willam Courtenay required no encouragement to live a life of excess. He was a habitual philanderer, gambler and drinker. Once he had gained possession of Catherine he quickly tired of her and took delight in tormenting her by boasting of his affairs with other women. Drink makes some men turn aggressive and that was the impact it had on Courtenay. As a result he often hit her when he came home from his debaucheries, though he was always careful to ensure he didn't mark her face. He did not want others to know of his behaviour. One evening he returned home with his uncle, Lord Hazleworth. Both men had been drinking very heavily. They subjected Catherine to the most appalling treatment and then both men raped her. That's how she became with child. Which of them was the father it would be impossible to say.'

Trollope was horrified. If Farrell was speaking the truth, his sister had been ill represented in court. 'But why did this not come out in the trial?' he asked.

'Richard Farrell says that Lord Hazleworth had stories about her alleged scandalous behaviour leaked to the press and, to make doubly sure her version wasn't heard, he paid a handsome sum not only to Catherine's defence lawyer but also to her parents to ensure they did nothing to promote her cause.'

'Surely no parent, however bad, would agree to let their child hang?'

'They'd no desire to see their role in the marriage uncovered and, as far as they were concerned, their daughter had let them down by murdering the man who would one day have inherited his uncle's title and wealth.'

'So she did murder her husband?'

'Yes, she did. The day after she'd been raped she hoped that her husband would show some remorse at what he and his uncle had done. In fact he treated the whole thing as a lark and told her to expect more of the same because his uncle had particularly enjoyed the evening. She informed her parents of what had happened but they told her to bear whatever her husband did rather than face a divorce. She had no one else to turn to for help. She believed her brother was dead. A week or so later her husband and his uncle again came home after a heavy drinking session. This time she was prepared. She had armed herself with a knife to defend herself and she threatened to kill them both if they assaulted her again. In their drunken state they were not deterred and her defiance, if anything, aroused them more. They attacked her and, in the struggle, Courtenay was mortally stabbed. Her uncle had her arrested and covered up his and his nephew's behaviour by making her out to be a monstrous wife.'

Trollope's heart went out to the unfortunate woman. Catherine Farrell might have appeared hard and unfeeling to John Gaunt but the poor woman had undoubtedly been traumatized by all that had happened to her. 'It's hard to believe that both her husband and her parents could both be so monstrous!'

'Richard Farrell told me that, although he'd given his whole life to spreading the gospel of Christ, he could not forgive his parents for their failure to defend his sister once they had finally confessed to him what had happened.'

'I'm amazed that Catherine Farrell showed such concern for a baby conceived in such circumstances.'

'It doesn't surprise me, Mr Trollope. I'm a doctor and, although I've not come across any case as bad as this one, I've seen many women give birth in situations where you would think they would hate the child. Most do not. They see the child for what it is – innocent of any of the events that have led to its birth.'

'Why have you told none of this to the Hardings?'

Bold suddenly looked very abashed and for a moment Trollope thought he was not going to answer the question. However, the young surgeon drew breath and blurted out, 'Because I feared that what Farrell had told me would simply cause unnecessary pain.'

'What on earth do you mean?'

'If I told Eleanor what I've told you, I know what her response would be – she'd immediately want to set the record straight, and, to do that, she'd make known the family's connection with Catherine Farrell. I firmly believe that the outcome of such a disclosure would not be the murderess's vindication but the destruction of the Hardings and Grantlys. Think about it, Mr Trollope! Why should the courts and the media take up the case of Catherine Farrell when it would compromise their own handling of the trial all those years ago? They'll simply say that Richard Farrell has invented all this in the hope of restoring his sister's reputation. He's no proof of what he says. His parents are dead and he destroyed the letters that Catherine wrote to him. They were too painful a reminder of his failure to protect her. The other key player, Lord Hazleworth, is also dead – not that he would condemn himself and his nephew by telling the truth if he were alive. Can't you see that it's better that the Harding family remain in ignorance of what Richard Farrell told me?'

'But surely if Catherine Farrell's reputation could be restored it would help the situation in which the family find themselves. To be her child would be far less a source of scandal for either Eleanor or Susan if their potential mother was not the cold-hearted murderess that she was thought to be.'

Bold shook his head. 'It's not as simple as that. If by some miracle we persuaded people to believe the story of Richard Farrell, we would do so by making them see that the child's father was one of two men, both of whom were monstrously evil. Catherine Farrell's child would still be judged tainted. Moreover, there would be some who would still condemn Catherine as a murderess, whatever provocation she faced. Whether we like it or not, tongues would wag just as maliciously if the truth about what happened all those years ago was known.'

Trollope stiffened but he knew that Bold's assumption was correct. 'The Bible says the sins of parents will fall upon their children,' he said sadly. 'This is one occasion when I wish that were not so. I can see why you've not informed the Hardings about what Richard Farrell told you, but what did you say to him?'

'That I believed him but that as he had no evidence I could do nothing with his story to restore his sister's reputation.'

'And he accepted that?'

'Why should he not? He'd come to the same conclusion years ago.'

'Better let sleeping dogs lie?'

Bold nodded.

9

THE DEVIL'S SIGN

TROLLOPE RETURNED TO his room within the warden's house. There he carefully read twice through the letters Bold had given him but to no purpose; they did not provide anything else worth following up. However, the more he thought about what he had just been told by Bold, the more he wondered why John Gaunt had informed Richard Farrell that his sister's child was dead. Was it simply that he had judged she would be better off with Mr Harding? If so, why? Surely he had not judged Richard Farrell tainted by his relationship with the murderess? The man was a respectable cleric. Could there be some other reason for Gaunt's lie? And, if so, did it shed any light on which of Mr Harding's daughters was Catherine Farrell's child? Trollope decided that he would have to clarify the matter with the former gaoler.

A few minutes later he was knocking on Gaunt's door. He waited a few minutes and, having received no reply, entered the room. The first thing he saw was the old man lying slumped in a chair and he immediately assumed that the murderer had struck again. However, he then noted the slow rise and fall of the man's chest and realized that Gaunt was simply fast asleep. It only took a gentle shake to rouse him. Trollope then proceeded to outline to him the version of events provided by Richard Farrell. Gaunt listened intently, without trying at any stage to interrupt.

'If what her brother says is true,' he said, once he had heard everything, 'I'll not deny the poor woman was as much sinned against as sinning, but nothing condones her murdering her husband. Nor can we be certain that Mr Farrell is speaking the truth. He didn't say anything about it to me when we met all those years ago. Why this dramatic change in his view? I'm still inclined to think the courts were correct in their judgement of her evil character.'

'I doubt whether the poor man was thinking very clearly when he met you,' responded Trollope. 'He must have been in a terrible state of mind at having arrived in England too late to do anything. Remember that he'd only just learned of his sister's death and didn't yet know the full circumstances surrounding her crime. His parents had taken payment to lie about what had happened. He'd not yet had the opportunity to drag out the truth from them about the events leading to his sister's arrest and conviction.'

'I can see you may be right,' conceded Gaunt, nodding his head.

'Why did you tell him that Catherine's child was dead? Was it that you judged the whole family evil?'

Surprise flickered across the old man's face. 'No, I saw nothing wrong with the gentleman and I respected his calling and the missionary work in which he was engaged. I informed him that Catherine Farrell's child had died because that was what I'd been told.'

'By whom?'

'By the wet nurse who'd taken her.'

This totally unexpected reply threw Trollope into confusion. 'But you no longer think that was the case because you told me one of Mr Harding's daughters is the child,' he stated.

'Yes, because a couple of years afterwards I received a brief note from Mr Harding saying that the child was now in his care and thanking me for my role in recommending the woman who had initially cared for her.'

'Did you not think to tell Richard Farrell?'

'I had no address for him or Mr Harding.'

'Tell me more about the wet nurse,' commanded Trollope.

'She was called Mrs Mather and her husband was a dockworker. I chose her on the recommendation of a gaoler friend of mine called Tom Paterson. He'd known her for a number of years. He said that she would be more suitable than most because of her educated background. According to Tom, her father was a prosperous shopkeeper called William Applecart and, as a child, she'd known what it was to have a good home and live in comfort. Unfortunately the real brains behind the family business was her mother and when she unexpectedly died from contracting a fever everything began going wrong. Applecart was far too kind a man. He allowed too many of his customers to run up debts they couldn't pay and so he went bankrupt. The loss of his shop broke his heart. As a result he died shortly afterwards, leaving his young daughter with hardly a penny to her name. All she possessed were her good looks and with these she got herself a husband, but not one from a wealthy background.'

'I don't understand. Why would this Mrs Mather have told you the child had died when it had not? Were you not angry at her deceit?'

'Yes, I was furious, but then I heard from Tom how her husband had taken to the drink and lost his job. That meant the family were entirely dependent on the money they were receiving from Mr Harding. He told me she'd lied rather than see the child taken away from her by Richard Farrell and begged me to forgive her.'

The explanation made sense to Trollope. He knew many women were driven to far worse than lying by their poverty. 'And do you have any idea where Mrs Mather is now?' he enquired.

'None whatsoever, but why do you ask?'

'Because Mr Harding deliberately ensured that he should not know which of his daughters was the child of his wife and which the child of Catherine Farrell. It's just possible that Mrs Mather may know of some identifying feature – a mole or other birthmark – that may help us identify which is which.'

John Gaunt was stunned. 'What father would do such a thing?' he gasped. 'Not to know your true child!'

'He did it because he wanted to make sure he'd show the same love to both girls.'

The bedesman disapprovingly shook his head. 'But it's made no difference, has it? Thomas Rider and Jeremiah Smith have both died at the hands of Catherine Farrell's child.'

'We've no proof that the murders were committed by either of the warden's daughters.'

'Evil blood will show itself. The mother committed murder. So has her child.'

Trollope was exasperated by the man's prejudice yet could not help feeling the man might be right. He contented himself with saying, 'Then all the more reason for seeking out this Mrs Mather to see if she can help us identify her.'

'You don't need Mrs Mather to tell you that information. I can tell you that. The baby carried the devil's mark.'

'What on earth do you mean?' exploded Trollope.

The bedesman looked pityingly at him as if despairing of his ignorance. ''Tis well known, sir, that the devil marks those who serve him. That's how they used to seek out witches in the old days.'

'Yes, and many an innocent woman was tortured and burned simply because she had some scar or blemish that had nothing to do with the devil!' retorted Trollope, amazed that an educated man like Gaunt should be so superstitious.

'Say what you like, sir. The Bible says the devil marks his own and he marked Catherine's child.'

Trollope knew it would be pointless to try and change the old man's mind. Instead he asked, 'In what way was she marked?'

'There was a brown mark on the infant's chest just

161

below the left nipple.'

'Then we've only to ask which of Mr Harding's daughters carries such a mark and we'll know the identity of Catherine Farrell's child!'

'Yes, and the killer of poor Thomas Rider and Jeremiah Smith.'

Keen to share his newfound knowledge, Trollope immediately set off to find Mr Harding. The warden was in his study and he listened avidly to the information that John Bold had acquired from Richard Farrell, though he was upset that his young friend had also become party to the family's secret. The account of the way Catherine Farrell had been treated by her husband visibly moved him. So too did Gaunt's revelation that her child carried a distinguishing birthmark. His voice slightly wavered as he sought to convey his feelings to Trollope.

'The poor woman sinned in what she did but my heart went out to her when I heard her confession all those years ago. I understood why she felt even God had deserted her. All she said is verified by Richard Farrell's account. She suffered much and there was no one to protect her. My decision to assist her child was unquestionably the right one.'

'Even if the child has become a killer?'

'That is by no means proven. We misjudged the mother. Let us not make the same mistake with her daughter.'

'So which of your daughters is her child? Which carries the birthmark?' asked Trollope impatiently.

'I don't know, Mr Trollope. I never saw either child naked. A nurse always saw to their physical needs when they were young.'

'But Dr Grantly will know if his wife bears such a mark.'

Mr Harding blushed. 'We can't assume that. She may have prevented him seeing the blemish if she possesses it.'

'Then the only sure way to find out is for you to ask Eleanor and Susan which of them carries a blemish on her breast.'

'I'm not sure I can ask such an indelicate question,' stammered the warden.

'For heaven's sake, sir, why not? You cannot wish for both of them to live their lives under a constant shadow.'

Mr Harding clutched at his imaginary violincello and struck several savage chords to give vent to his anguish. 'So I must save one by ruining the reputation of the other? And I must discover the one thing I promised never to know – which of them is not of my blood?' he intoned. 'You ask too much of me, Mr Trollope.'

'Must I remind you that two men have been murdered because they knew of the existence of Catherine Farrell's child? For all we know others may be at risk, including John Gaunt,' countered Trollope. 'I know that we can't assume that Catherine's daughter is the killer we seek, but we can't turn our back on the one clue we have.'

The warden's playing ceased as abruptly as it had started and he sank into a chair. He wrapped his hands around the back of his head as he lowered his face till it almost touched his knees. Sobs rent his body. Trollope had not the heart to continue placing further pressure on him. He placed one hand gently on Mr Harding's head and wordlessly prayed that the poor man might be given the strength to do what was necessary. It took a few minutes for the warden to cease weeping. Slowly he raised his tear-stained face and said in a voice that was wracked with pain, 'I fear you're right, Mr Trollope, and I'll do as you ask.' He paused to try and control his trembling. 'All I ask is that I first share with my daughters the truth about what led to Catherine Farrell's murder of her husband. Whichever of them has her as her mother deserves to know that her crime was the product of the cruelties inflicted on her.'

'I think that's a good idea,' said Trollope, relieved at the outcome, 'but we must not forget that John Bold didn't want what he was told by Richard Farrell revealed.'

'Then I'll persuade him otherwise. Indeed, I think it right that both he and Dr Grantly should be present when I put the question of the birthmark to both my daughters. Both gentlemen have a strong vested interest in the outcome!'

'And what about me?'

'My courage may fail me so I want you there. If necessary you can take over telling them what we know. All I ask is that you do not yet divulge anything to Inspector Blake. He would probably want to place whichever is Catherine Farrell's daughter under immediate arrest.'

Trollope nervously wiped his mouth. 'There'll come a time soon when we'll have to divulge everything to him but I'll honour your request.'

'Then I suggest that you go and fetch Mr Bold whilst I gather my family. Let us all aim to be present in the drawing room by six o'clock. By then the inspector will have definitely left Hiram's for the day. Agreed?'

'Agreed.'

There was an air of curious alarm when the six people gathered in the parlour at the appointed time. By then, Trollope had cleared with John Bold that he should speak about what Richard Farrell had said. Mr Harding was too emotional to initiate the conversation and so it was left to Trollope to outline what he had learned about Catherine Farrell. He requested that Bold should confirm his account. The doctor nodded and Trollope then told them about the revelation from John Gaunt and how Catherine Farrell's child had a distinguishing birthmark on her chest. The eyes of all four men turned on the two women.

'One of you knows you carry a mark,' said Mr Harding, breaking his silence as he gazed painfully at the two women he loved most in the world. 'Do you want to inform us? Or would you prefer us to remain in ignorance?'

'That's not an option we can afford,' interrupted Dr Grantly. 'We must know the truth, however painful that may be.'

The two sisters looked tentatively at each other as if gauging who should speak first. It was Mrs Grantly who opted to do so. 'Until this moment I knew not whether I was Catherine Farrell's child, but now I know the answer,' she said in a trembling voice. She stopped to stare lovingly at her husband. 'You said that you loved me regardless of my ancestry. I'll never forget that. No man could have shown more loyalty and love to a wife than you've done.' Dr Grantly stared back at her, fearing the worst. She smiled reassuringly and held out her arms to him. 'My dearest, I'm pleased to say that your strength will not have to be tested.' She smiled. 'I'm not the daughter of Catherine Farrell. I carry no birthmark.'

Dr Grantly did not need to speak to show his joy. His face lit up. The burden that had weighed him down dropped from his shoulders. He rushed to put his arms around his wife. However, his delight was matched by John Bold's despair. Trollope appreciated that all his worst nightmares must have been suddenly realized. In the circumstances that had been uncovered, marriage to Eleanor would rule out any chance he might have of becoming a successful doctor in Barchester. As for Eleanor Harding, she stood as if she had been suddenly frozen to the spot.

Mrs Grantly disengaged herself from her husband and looked pityingly at the woman she had so long called her sister. 'I'm sorry, Eleanor,' she said and her voice sounded brittle, 'but I couldn't let my husband live any longer in uncertainty. You know his position would be totally undermined in Barchester if it became common knowledge that I might be the child of a murderess.'

Mr Harding went over to Eleanor and gently took her hands in his. 'This makes no difference to our love,' he whispered. 'I still love you. In my eyes you are as much my child as you ever were.'

She squeezed his hands and fought to hold back the tears that his kind words evoked. Biting her lips, she struggled to retain her composure. Then she said what none of them expected to hear. 'Thank you, Papa, but I've no need of your compassion. You mistake my silence for admission.' She turned to the others in the room. 'When Mr Trollope said Catherine Farrell's child possessed a blemish, I inwardly breathed a sigh of relief because I knew I carried no such mark on my skin. Naturally that pleasure was quickly replaced with sorrow for my sister's position. I drew the obvious conclusion. What was good news for me must be very bad news for her. That's why I was so stunned when she stated she also bore no birthmark.'

'What! Neither of you possess a birthmark on your skin?' gasped Trollope.

Both women nodded.

Dr Grantly almost wept in frustration. 'Then this meeting has been a wild goose chase! John Gaunt's memory was clearly at fault on this matter.'

'Not necessarily,' interrupted Trollope. 'There is another explanation.'

'Well, for the life of me I can't see it,' grumbled the archdeacon.

'John Gaunt told Richard Farrell that his infant niece had died. He got that information from the child's nurse, but she subsequently told his friend, Tom Paterson, that she'd lied. However, what if she told the truth the first time? What if Catherine's child, the child with the birthmark, had died? Many infants do.'

'I'm at a complete loss to understand what you

mean,' complained Mr Harding. 'How can that be when I took the child into my home?'

'I know exactly what he means,' responded Dr Grantly, whose sharp mind had suddenly grasped what Trollope was thinking. 'The child that was given to you was not Catherine Farrell's child. That had died. The child given to you had some other mother as its parent.'

'But that makes no sense!'

'It makes eminent sense,' Trollope contradicted. 'Mrs Mather never told you of the child's death because, by letting you live in ignorance, she remained in receipt of good money for looking after a child that no longer existed. Imagine her horror when you suddenly asked to have the child returned to you. Rather than face the consequences of her deceit, she found another child to give you.'

'But where would she get it from?'

'I can assure you that there are plenty of unwanted children in London. She would have found no problem in finding a substitute.'

Eleanor Harding's eyes flashed angrily at this exchange. 'So what you're saying is that one of us is just an unwanted child plucked from a workhouse or worse? I for one would prefer to be Catherine Farrell's child. At least I would then have had a mother who loved me.'

'Don't be foolish, sister,' interrupted Mrs Grantly. 'I'd much rather have an unknown mother than a criminal one. Moreover, there are plenty of women who give up their child not from lack of love but out of necessity. Maybe the mother of one of us thought her child would be better cared for in the home of a kindly man.'

'There's one thing for sure – the only way of knowing the origin of one of you is to find Mrs Mather,' uttered John Bold, who was finding it hard to disguise the extent of his own emotion. 'If you wish it, I'm willing to spend time seeing if she's still alive.'

Dr Grantly shook his head. 'That's a typical hot-headed response! It's in all our interests to live in ignorance. No one can cast a stone against a mother who is unknown. Let us just rejoice in the fact that the shadow of Catherine Farrell no longer hangs over this household.'

'I'm sorry but it's not that simple,' said Trollope. 'Her shadow remains because the murders took place before we learnt what we now know. The inspector, if he hears of all this, will judge that all of you had good reason to want the two bedesmen silenced.'

'I cannot bear this anymore!' shouted out Mr Harding angrily. 'You make it sound as if all this family cares about is its reputation!' For once there was no recourse to his violincello. A look of quiet determination settled on his face as he glared at the others in the room. 'I'm tired of deceit. With every passing minute I realize that it was very wrong of me to engage in it all those years ago. Why should I have been afraid of telling the world that I had adopted Catherine Farrell's child? It was an act of kindness and is not that what the gospel demands of us? Why should I have been afraid that I might love the child less? Are there not countless adopted children who are deeply loved by those who have brought them into the bosom of their family?'

No one spoke but Trollope's heart went out to the man. He had thought earlier in the day that Mr Harding was a broken man. Yet now his manner was almost like that of an ancient prophet, strong and resolute.

'I think the time has come for us all to do what is right and not what is convenient,' Mr Harding continued. 'How can we continue to pervert the cause of justice by refusing to tell what we know to the inspector? Do we not wish the person who murdered poor Thomas Rider and Jeremiah Smith to be caught? Does not our Lord call on us to be speakers of truth? I confess that I have permitted my judgement to be corrupted by my love for my daughters, but no more, no more!' His voice cracked and the pain that underlay his courage was momentarily evident. Pulling himself together, he concluded, 'Tomorrow morning Mr Blake must be told everything. Let him decide what he does with the information. If he chooses to tell our story to the press, so be it. We will face what must be faced together!'

'Don't be a fool, Papa. You risk shaming us all,' snapped back Mrs Grantly.

'I disagree,' replied Trollope. 'I think your father's right. The most important thing now is not hiding that either you or your sister has an unknown mother. It's finding out who killed Thomas Rider and Jeremiah Smith. Until that happens there's not a person in this room who will be free of suspicion.'

Dr Grantly could not help grimacing but he concurred with what Trollope had said. 'I've no great faith in the ability of Inspector Blake,' he muttered, 'but our decision earlier today was wrong. We must tell him what we know.'

'It's agreed then?' asked the warden, his strength almost done.

One by one the others grimly gave their assent, all except Mrs Grantly. 'I pray that you don't live to regret this!' she said and she stormed out of the room, slamming the door behind her.

'I'll go to her. She's understandably distraught,' said her husband. 'I'm sure that she'll come round to accepting our decision.' The others could see that this was said more in hope than expectation.

Neither Mrs Grantly nor Eleanor Harding chose to be present when Inspector Blake arrived very early the next day. Mrs Winthrop took him to the study where Mr Harding, Dr Grantly and Trollope were awaiting him. Between them they relayed all that they knew. Understandably he was not amused that he had been kept in the dark for so long but he was sufficiently astute to understand the motives of the family and grateful that they had finally decided to take him into their confidence. He at once asked that he should first be permitted to speak with John Gaunt in case he could extract anything else that might be useful and then that there should be a meeting in the parlour later in the morning with not only all Mr Harding's family present but also John Bold and Anthony Trollope. It was agreed that Trollope would fetch Bold for that purpose.

The meeting began at eleven and the inspector took

the lead throughout. 'I want you all to know that I do understand the delicacy of the situation that you're in,' he commenced reassuringly. 'That's why so far I've kept all information about these crimes out of the hands of the press by insisting that no bedesman leaves the premises.' If he had expected appreciation he saw none in their faces and he frowned. 'I warn you that I can't keep Barchester from knowing what has happened for much longer. It's most unfortunate that so much of my time has been wasted by you not being more open with me from the outset. By now we might have resolved these crimes.'

'We made an error of judgement, Mr Blake, for which I take responsibility,' answered Mr Harding wearily. 'We should have trusted you earlier as indeed Mr Trollope advised.'

The inspector acknowledged the apology with a slight inclination of his head and then pressed on. 'I'm not going to dwell on the details of this case now. You know them already. The motive for murdering both men appears obvious – to avoid a family scandal. I think that we can safely assume that these murders wouldn't have occurred had it been known that neither of Mr Harding's daughters has Catherine Farrell as a mother.' He paused to give added weight to what he was about to say. 'For that reason you must all accept that, with the exception of Mr Trollope, the people in this room are those with the most vested interest in committing the crimes. No one else has such a strong motive.'

'I agree with your logic but I don't believe one of us is guilty,' responded Dr Grantly promptly.

'But that's not what the world will think when it hears what has happened here,' Blake argued fiercely.

Mrs Grantly audibly drew breath and scowled at him. 'Not necessarily. My father is a much loved and respected man. People will accept that one of the bedesmen may have killed to protect him.' She looked to her husband to support what she had said but he remained ominously silent.

'I fear they're more likely to judge that all the bedesmen are too frail to be murderers,' pointed out the inspector.

'That's ridiculous!' she said, trying to retain her temper. 'Some of them are still active enough to wield a knife effectively, especially when that blade is directed into an unsuspecting victim.'

'There is some truth in what you say,' admitted Bold, anxious to avoid a situation in which the inspector's goodwill might be lost, 'but people will prefer the more scandalous possibilities.'

The inspector welcomed the young doctor's support but was not satisfied that the gravity of the situation had yet fallen on the family. 'Let us agree on one thing,' he said gravely. 'The murderer has to be someone at Hiram's. A stranger would have been spotted and the fact both murdered men appear to have died without a struggle points to them knowing – but possibly not suspecting – their killer. Do you all accept that?'

All heads nodded.

'In that case, I must ask for your patience while I continue to interrogate everybody further – and by that I mean not just again asking questions of the remaining bedesmen but also seeking answers from all of you with the exception of Mr Trollope.' He saw the surprise this evoked and quickly explained why. 'Last night I received confirmation that he is who he says he is and I totally accept that his involvement here has been entirely accidental. For that reason he is free to leave Hiram's Hospital.'

Trollope welcomed the news that he was no longer a suspect but he was sorry he was leaving behind a family in turmoil. 'If I can do anything to help I'm willing to stay on if my employers will permit it.'

'That will not be necessary,' retorted Mrs Grantly ungraciously. 'We don't require your assistance.'

'I think you may help more by returning to London,' said the inspector before anyone else could respond. He saw the puzzlement on Trollope's face and added, 'I don't want to waste my time seeking this woman called Mather and I'm happy to delegate the task to you if you'll promise to undertake it.'

'Involve the police and they instantly pass on their responsibilities to others!' snorted Mrs Grantly.

'I'm sure the inspector has his reasons,' intervened Eleanor Harding.

'Yes, I have. I'm not convinced that there is much of value to be obtained from pursuing the woman who foisted on to Mr Harding an unknown child twenty years ago. How will that help identify our murderer? I would much prefer to spend my time asking questions of everyone connected to Hiram's Hospital than travel on some silly goose chase to London. You're clutching at straws if you think discovering the true parentage of one of Mr Harding's daughters will lead to an alternative line of investigation.'

'You don't make it sound an inviting task for me to undertake,' Trollope commented.

'It's not, but it's also not difficult. All you have to do is go to Newgate Prison and see if Gaunt's former associate, Tom Paterson, knows where Mrs Mather now lives. If you get her address you can go and see her.'

'But surely all that is better done by you?'

'No. It's better that you should do it for two simple reasons. First, as I have already said, I think my time would be better served here. Secondly, and perhaps more importantly, it means that if you do discover information about the child you need only inform the people in this room. If I undertake the task, I would have to incorporate that information into my official report, even if it was not relevant to the murders, and I can't guarantee that such a report would not eventually find its way into the hands of the press.'

Trollope at once saw the sense in what the inspector was saying.

'Will you do this for us?' asked Mr Harding.

'Willingly.'

'Good!' said the inspector. 'Then I'll write a letter for you to take to the turnkey at Newgate Prison, requesting that he assist you, and I suggest you head back to London this afternoon.'

'I'll go on the railway. It's much faster,' responded Trollope. 'Once I've seen my employers, I'll go at once to Newgate. Then I can return here and let you know the outcome before I collect my horses and resume my work.'

10

THE PRISON AND THE WORKHOUSE

TROLLOPE NEVER FOUND walking through the crowded streets of London a pleasurable experience because of the shoving and pushing that took place and the constant stream of invective that filled the air. In the busy areas strangers paid no heed to the comfort of others and it was not uncommon for accidental jostling to lead to an exchange of kicks and blows without compunction. Nor was it enjoyable to see everywhere around you in fellow travellers such striking evidence of poverty and disease. There were few who did not bear signs of the hardships they had endured – bodies twisted by rickets or inhumanly maimed by the hazards of employment, faces ravaged by the scars of smallpox or other diseases. What made his journey even worse was that he had to cross so many roads and no vehicle stopped for any pedestrian. Instead the air rang with the neighing of horses and the rattle of ironshod wheels as drivers sought to drive their vehicles over the cobbled streets regardless of the safety of him or anyone else.

Nor were these the only reasons he disliked the city. The air was almost always soot-filled and there was a constant stench that arose from the mass unwashed and the multitude of industries that operated in the polluted streets: forges, foundries, breweries, tanneries and the like. Trollope was particularly glad when he had passed through Smithfield and no longer had to endure its slaughterhouse smells or, worse still, listen to the squealing of animals being butchered. Everything in the market's vicinity seemed smeared with either fat or blood. He turned into a street and saw ahead of him Newgate Prison and behind it the great dome of St Paul's Cathedral. Straw had been placed on the ground to deaden the noise of passing vehicles – a sure sign that trials were taking place in the Sessions House that had been built next to the forbidding fortress. He pressed on, forcing his way through the vast crowd that had gathered round Newgate's grey, filth-encrusted walls. Most of the people reeked of spirits and beer.

Trollope could not help shuddering as he showed the inspector's letter to a guard and sought admittance. The prison's huge gates and gratings bore witness to the fact that few who entered its walls as prisoners were ever expected to regain their freedom. Once inside, he was taken up a flight of narrow stairs to the turnkey's room by an ill-dressed lad. Sparsely furnished, it looked more like a cell than an office and its occupier was a grim-faced man of forbidding aspect. His face looked neither clean nor wholesome, partly because his mouth and chin bristled with stubble and partly because his dark sunken eyes looked restless and cunning. He lacked any of the grace of manner that had characterized John Gaunt. Trollope handed over the letter of introduction that Blake had given him. He had seen its contents and knew the inspector had chosen his words carefully. The letter contained no reference to the Hardings or the events at Hiram's Hospital. It merely stated that the police were keen to discover precisely what had happened to the child of a convicted murderess called Catherine Courtenay, better known as Catherine Farrell.

The turnkey opened the letter and slowly read it. He sniffed, rubbed the side of his bulbous nose with the back of his left hand, and then spat onto the floor. Trollope could not help but notice how very dirty his hands were. 'We've enough to do here, sir, dealing with the living and those about to die without worrying about the offspring of someone who was hung 'ere twenty or more years ago,' the man said in an irritated tone.

'I really will not take up much of your time,' responded Trollope. 'All I want to know is whether there is anyone here who might recall John Gaunt and one associated with him, a gaoler friend called Tom Paterson.'

'Aye, there's a few here who knew John and that includes me. I took on his job when he left. He was a good man. As for Tom Paterson, he still works here, though that's more out of charity than anything else. He's too old and crippled with arthritis to undertake much of use. We keep him busy by letting him run errands for those prisoners who have the money to purchase things and so make their stay a little more pleasant. But what's Paterson got to do with all this?' He waved the letter of introduction that he had been given.

'John Gaunt was the gaoler of Catherine Farrell and he arranged for her infant daughter to be cared for by a woman called Mrs Mather. Tom Paterson recommended her. My hope is that he or someone else here might know her current whereabouts. We need to find this Mrs Mather so she can hopefully tell us exactly what happened all those years ago.'

'But why are the police interested in finding a murderess's child after all these years?' enquired the turnkey.

'Because her brother was told by Gaunt that the child had died but now Gaunt says he was misinformed.'

'I don't know anything about that. I was but a young man when Catherine Farrell was hung. However, her I can recall. Pretty she was. Face like an angel.'

'So I've been told.'

The turnkey grinned. 'She didn't look so angel-like when the hangman had finished with 'er. I helped cut 'er down.' He stood up and took a large bunch of keys out from a drawer in his desk. 'I can't imagine any child of hers will have come to much good after all these years if it has survived, but I'll take you to Tom Paterson. He should be working in the men's yard.'

He led Trollope down an ill-lit passage into a small open court. It was surrounded by high walls and dominated by a large building with iron-grated windows. He informed his visitor that this was where the female prisoners were held but did not offer to show Trollope around. Instead they passed on through several rooms and corridors until they arrived at a set of three court-yards, which acted as the exercise yards for the male prisoners. A number of men were there but there was no sign of any activity on their part to keep fit. They loitered in corners and occasionally glared inso-lently at the guards on duty. Sometimes one or two exchanged conversation with each other but, from the little that was audible, the subject matter was far from edifying. Everything about their manner was unsavoury. The only exception appeared to be a very young lad, who was on his own and obviously terri-fied. The turnkey saw Trollope looking in his direction and offered a word of explanation. 'He's new. He'll soon learn the ways of this place.'

'I thought the aim of prison was to deter people from crime?'

'So some say. People like to see criminals locked up for their crimes. It makes them feel happier and helps them pretend that the world is a just place. But I tell you, prison usually only corrupts men and women more. In my experience those who leave here depart more vicious and more cunning than when they entered. The only thing they've learned is better ways of committing crime and their only resolve is not to be caught again.'

'Say what you like. I would rather die than have to live here,' muttered Trollope, rejecting the turnkey's cynicism as he stared up at the prison walls that sur-rounded him.

'Oh, it's not so bad, sir. That's why it's no deterrent.

The prisoners employ themselves as they please and they're well fed. Some better 'ere than outside. Each man gets a pint of thick gruel each morning and half a pound of meat or a mess of broth alternately for dinner, as well as a pound of bread each day. Each has a mattress and two blankets for sleeping and, in winter, there is coal to provide some warmth.'

'Until some of them have to face the hangman.'

The turnkey laughed and replied, 'There's worse ways of dying.' Shortly afterwards he pointed out an old man who was carrying some half bottles of gin. 'There's Tom Paterson. Come, we'll easily catch him up. He moves pretty slowly because of his arthritis. I'll find us a room where there are no prisoners and we can talk with him in private.'

After introductions had been made, the three men made their way into one of the larger cells. It was a whitewashed room that was more airy than Trollope had expected, given the fact it was lit only by a window that looked into the courtyard they had left. Along both sides of the room ran a high shelf on which blankets were stored and from which a dozen sleeping mats were suspended by hooks. In the centre of the room was a deal table on which were a few pewter dishes. Around it were some benches. Paterson's frailty was evident in the way that he instantly placed the bottles of gin on the table and took the opportunity to sit down. He was skeleton-thin and it was obvious that parts of his body were severely crippled with arthritis. However, he uttered no word of complaint about his condition and smiled at Trollope. His haggard face had a natural honesty to it that Trollope found encouraging, given how long the man must have served within Newgate's grim confines.

'Mr Trollope is here representing the police,' explained the turnkey. 'They're acting on behalf of the brother of Catherine Farrell who was executed here over twenty years ago. This brother wants to know whether his niece – the murderess's child – died or not. John Gaunt told him she had but he now thinks the child survived. He says a woman called Mrs Mather should be able to confirm what actually happened. Mr Trollope's here to see if you might still know her whereabouts. Apparently you recommended her to John for the task of wet nurse.'

'Aye, I did,' Paterson replied in a voice that was more refined than that of the turnkey. 'A good woman she was and a pretty one.'

'What was your connection with her?' asked Trollope.

'When I was a young man I took quite a shine to her but she chose another. Alexander Mather was a fine man to look at but he had the devil in him when he got drunk – and that was too often for his good or hers. She deserved a better husband. I got her the job of looking after Catherine Farrell's child because she desperately needed the money. Her husband was not providing enough for her to feed herself or her family. I told John Gaunt that was because the man was ill but the only illness Alexander Mather had was his fondness for gin.'

'How many children did they have?' asked Trollope, keen to put Paterson at ease.

'Two sons and a daughter.'

'And are any of those alive?'

'I know that the two boys died because I comforted her as best I could when those deaths happened. I afterwards heard that the girl had also died.' The old man shrugged his shoulders and for the first time in their interview looked very uncomfortable. 'And I'm sorry to say it, sir, but I think you've had a wasted journey as far as Catherine Farrell's child is concerned. It died when it was still less than two years old. Mr Farrell was told the truth.'

'But that's not what Mrs Mather told the man who was paying her to look after it,' said Trollope in a tone designed to instill fear into the old gaoler.

For the first time Paterson looked apprehensive. 'I'm afraid that was her husband's fault. He didn't want to lose the money that was being paid for the child's upkeep.'

'And why did you go along with that lie?'

'I didn't want to get Mrs Mather into trouble. I'd seen the poverty in which she lived. What harm did the lie make? The money probably mattered little to the man who paid it and it meant everything to her.'

'When the man claimed the child, you let John Gaunt think he got Catherine Farrell's genuine daughter. You told him Mrs Mather's initial report of its death was a lie to ensure it was not taken away by its uncle.'

'I did,' said Paterson, looking very miserable.

'So whose child did she subsequently hand over?'

'I've no idea. She never told me and I'd no desire to know. I was content that the man got a child to love.'

'So what happened to Mrs Mather and her

husband?' asked Trollope, choosing not to voice any condemnation of the man's actions.

'She eventually left him,' said Paterson bluntly. 'I wasn't surprised. He treated her more and more badly. There were a number of times when I saw her and she couldn't cover the bruises, much though she tried. I've no idea where she is now. I lost all contact with her once she'd fled from her husband, though someone told me that they'd heard that her daughter died not long afterwards.'

'And what of her husband?'

'Alexander Mather still lives near here. I've had nothing to do with the man since his wife left him, but from what I've heard he's got what he deserves. He's a poor shadow of what he once was.'

'Can you tell me his address and give me directions to it?' asked Trollope, trying to disguise his excitement. There was every chance that Mrs Mather's husband would know from whence the child came.

'He's easy enough to find, sir, though I can't imagine he can tell you anything I've not. The poor soul's in the parish workhouse.' He shook his head and added, 'My one prayer is that I may never end up there.'

'Come now, Tom, you've plenty of life in you yet!' lied the turnkey.

Trollope thanked the two men for their assistance and slipped each of them a coin. Once he had been escorted back out of the prison, he set off for the workhouse that was Alexander Mather's home. He knew that the poor looked on entering one as the worst possible fate because it was workhouse policy to deliberately separate husband and wife, parent and child, brother and sister. Moreover, they forced their inmates to perform degrading tasks in a way that no prison did. However, like many men of his generation, Trollope's knowledge of such institutions was largely confined to what had been written about them in the books of Charles Dickens. In the event, the reality was worse than the fiction. To a sensitive mind like his the misery of the place was palpable and he tried to avert his gaze from the sight of so many people who had visibly lost all hope.

The overseer of the workhouse was a fat and cheery man who looked out of place in his surroundings. He told Trollope that Alexander Mather had recently become very sick and was in their infirmary. Leaning over, he confided in Trollope's ear, 'I think he's not got long to live, but he is still perfectly able to hold a conversation if he chooses to do so.' Stiffly he stood up and added, 'I'll escort you to see him if you like.'

The infirmary was a spacious but dim-lit room with beds arranged in two long rows on either side of it. Virtually all the beds were occupied but there was no sound from any of the sick, except for the wailing of an old woman who was beating her fist against the wall. Many of the occupants bore evidence of ill usage and it was obvious a number were near death. Their wan faces stared back at Trollope as if he might be the Grim Reaper come to collect them now they were hapless to resist his dark embrace. The overseer directed Trollope to a vacant bed at the far end of the room. Sitting on a chair next to it was the slumped figure of a man. This was Alexander Mather. By his calculations Trollope had been expecting to see someone in his forties or early fifties, but the man by the bed looked far older than that. If he had once been handsome, there was no remaining sign of it. Trollope judged that drink and disease had probably altered him beyond all recognition. Mather's grey hair was long and lank, his cheeks were pale and sunken, and spit dribbled from his mouth.

As Trollope drew up to him he could hear the man's laboured breathing and he saw in his rheumy eyes the kind of despair that he had last seen when looking into the eyes of a cornered fox which had exhausted itself fleeing the hounds. 'Mr Mather, my name's Anthony Trollope,' he said loudly in the hope of making the man hear what he said. 'I've come to ask you about your wife. Are you willing to talk with me?'

'I've no wife,' muttered the sick man feebly.

'But there was a time when you did.'

Mather seemed to struggle with this idea but then a glimmer of recognition appeared in his eyes as memories of her began to surface. A rather lewd look flitted across his face, and this was made more obscene when he leant across to whisper in Trollope's ear, 'She were a pretty woman, she were.'

'Where is she now?' asked Trollope, moving back a little and trying not to show his disgust.

Mather ignored the question, lost in a sudden flow of memories from his past. 'There were quite a few would 'ave liked to 'ave 'er, but it were me she chose,' he said proudly. 'I were quite a lad then. Me mother used to say that I 'ad the looks to charm the angels, let alone any woman.' His lips pursed into a rather supercilious sneer. 'We did it all proper too. She were far too well brought up to jist live with me. Married in church, we were, like the gentry.' He paused and a look of distaste flickered across his thin face. 'Not that any came from 'er family.'

'Why was that?' enquired Trollope, deciding he might get more out of the man if he let him remember the past in his own way.

'They thought she were too good fer me, me being jist a workin' man. Yet I was ready to look after 'er. They weren't. Left alone she was when 'er father died.'

'And were you happy?'

He did not respond immediately but then made a grimace and said in a hollow voice, 'At first, though I had to knock some of the airs and graces out of 'er. Make 'er know 'er place.'

Trollope dreaded to think what terrible deeds lay behind these words. Educated and brought up in a different world, she must have suffered much at her husband's hands.

'Then it all went wrong,' continued Mather.

'In what way?'

'We 'ad two sons, fine lads they were, but she let 'em take sick with the scarlet fever. She nursed 'em for day after day but they both died.' From the expression on his face it was obvious that he still found the memory of their loss painful. 'It's 'ard to see yer sons lying cold and stiff,' he murmured, 'and so I took to the drink. I sought to drown me sorrows in gin. After that things got bad between us, 'specially when I ceased getting work because the drink made me unreliable. She promised me another son but the silly cow gave birth to a girl. What use was that to me?'

'How did you live if you had no employment to bring in money?' asked Trollope, trying not to show his revulsion at the man's uncharitable words.

'I told 'er she should make 'erself available.'

'Available?'

'To men. She were still a pretty woman. I needed money for drink and she'd only to open her legs to get it fer me. But she wouldn't, not 'er, not even when I hit 'er. Right stubborn she were.'

Trollope was shocked that there was not a hint of any regret or remorse that he had asked his wife to become a prostitute; just anger at her refusal to obey him.

'She took in washing and did other work instead, though that brought in precious little,' continued Mather, clearly oblivious of the bad impression he was creating. 'She even took in some man's child in return for money, not that I wanted another brat near me. I told 'er to keep the two girls quiet or I'd shake 'em so 'ard they'd nivver bawl agin.'

'What happened to the child your wife took in?'

'It fell sick and died. I was mad when she told the prison that. I told 'er not to be so stupid and to make sure its father nivver 'eard about it. That way we'd get paid without the expense of looking arter it.'

'And what happened to your daughter?'

'My wife took 'er away when she left me.'

'Why did she leave you?'

For a moment a fire returned to Mather's eyes. He moved to bring himself closer to Trollope with an unexpected energy and said with venom in his voice, "Twas cos I cut 'er.'

Trollope looked puzzled. 'I don't understand. What do you mean?'

Mather fell back into his chair, cast an eye around him as if checking no one else could hear, and then replied in a foul-breathed whisper, 'I'd taken money fer drink as was me right and she dared swear at me when I returned home late. Said didn't I realize that the money from the dead child's father was due to come to an end and that I was starving 'er and our child and that I'd left 'er with nothing fer the rent.' His voice rose as he confided what he had said in reply. 'I told 'er to pay the landlord in other ways. I'd seen him ogling at 'er. Easy pickings he were.' His right hand grabbed hold of Trollope's arm and he pulled him towards him. 'A wife's there to see to 'er husband's needs and do what he wants. Ain't that right? That's what the Bible says. Honour and obey she promised.'

Trollope did not say anything but he sensed that Mather took his silence for assent. 'She got up and took a knife from the table and dared threaten me,' the old man continued. 'She said she'd rather use 'er looks to find another 'usband so I seized the knife from 'er and I told 'er I'd see that no man would want to 'ave her as a wife. I then cut 'er good and proper.' He smirked and moved the forefinger of his right hand up to his face and drew a line down his left cheek. 'Next morning she and the child were gone. I nivver saw 'em again.'

Trollope offered neither reproach nor recrimination but his mind reeled, not just at the horror of what had been described but at what the former dockworker's story had led him to surmise. Mather had scarred his wife's left cheek and Mrs Winthrop, the housekeeper at Hiram's Hospital, had such a scar. Was that a mere coincidence or was it possible that Mrs Winthrop was Mrs Mather? Once she had fled her husband, there would have been every reason for her to pass off her own daughter as the child of Catherine Farrell. How else would she have been able to ensure its welfare? She could easily have given out to others that her daughter had died. By handing the child over, she ensured that it would be brought up comfortably.

It was not too difficult to surmise how Mrs Mather had eventually come into the service of Mr Harding. His arrangements for the collection of the two girls had not been complex. She could easily have changed her name and secretly followed her daughter's sub-sequent movements and, because of her educated background, found employment in Barchester. She had then become Mr Harding's housekeeper when the opportunity arose. What better way to have daily contact with her child? The more he thought about it the more this seemed to make sense and, if it were true, Trollope realized it gave Mrs Winthrop perhaps the strongest motive to commit the killings at Hiram's Hospital. Had Thomas Rider somehow discovered Mrs Winthrop's true identity? Or was it simply that Mrs Winthrop had feared he would tell the world that one of the daughters of the warden was Catherine Farrell's child and, in the process, wreck the happiness she had worked so long to create for her own child?

Trollope knew he had to get back to Barchester as quickly as he could and tell the inspector and the Hardings what he had uncovered. Mrs Winthrop must become the prime suspect if Mr Harding did not possess good reasons as to why his housekeeper could not possibly be Mrs Mather. Trollope left the workhouse as speedily as politeness permitted and purchased a copy of *Bradshaw's Monthly Railway Guide*. He discovered that the earliest train he could catch in the morning on the London and South Western Railway would get him to Barchester by just before eleven o'clock. As he headed back to the hotel where he intended to stay for the night, a sudden depressing thought occurred to him. If Mrs Winthrop were guilty, it would make one of the warden's two daughters the child of a murderess! His heart sank. He suddenly saw that what he had discovered was likely to expose the entire family to the most scandalous rumours when the matter became public.

11

A MOTHER'S LOVE

MRS WINTHROP WAS not a happy woman. For years she had forgotten what it felt like to be so miserable, even though there were days when she still grieved for the loss of her two boys. At the time she had bitterly resented her husband blaming her for their deaths, but gradually she had come to see it was his way of dealing with a grief that was as deep as hers. He had not been able to grasp why he should have lost two strong sons unless her nursing was at fault. She had been more fortunate than him. In her case the passing years had eased her sorrow because she had been able to watch her daughter grow and flourish, first from a distance, and then, once she entered Mr Harding's service, on a daily basis. It did not matter that her child did not know her to be her mother.

Surely her decision all those years ago had been the right one? If she had stayed with her husband, she dreaded to think what would have become of her daughter and her. The combination of drink and despair had turned him into a monster. Their flight had caused him no pain because their presence had brought him no pleasure, only resentment. It had long been her wish that he might have become a better man again after her flight. He had come to rely on the money she earned for drink. Had he been forced to take up work again? Had he found himself a new wife? Had he new sons to take a pride in? She hoped so. In recent years she had grown accustomed to thinking of him more as he had been when he had courted her. The time before drink took hold of him. Her own happiness at watching her daughter's development had progressively dimmed the memory of her suffering at his hands, even though the livid scar on her cheek was a constant reminder of his brutality.

Pretending that her daughter was Catherine Farrell's had caused no one to suffer. Quite the reverse. If she had reported the real child's death, she would have simply condemned Mr Harding to a life of remorse at his failure to protect her. Knowing his kind heart, he would have felt forever guilty that he had not taken the infant straight into his home in accordance with his promise. Had not the presence of her daughter also given much happiness to Mr Harding's true child? Susan and Eleanor might only be sisters in name but the two children had grown up thinking they were of the same blood. Their relationship was as close as any parent could possibly wish for their children.

It was John Gaunt's return to Barchester that had changed everything so badly, though not for the reasons that she had initially feared. She had met him but once before – at the time when he handed over Catherine Farrell's child into her care – and the disfiguring scar on her left cheek and many years of constant work had rendered too much change in her appearance for him to recognize her. Moreover, his loyalty and love for Mr Harding had prevented him speaking to anyone in Barchester of what had happened at Newgate all those years ago. As month succeeded month, her fears had gradually subsided. But old men like to talk and Gaunt had proved no exception. He had eventually told Mr Harding's secret to his friend, Thomas Rider, on a day when the two old men were exchanging stories about the warden's innate kindness to others. She supposed he had decided to do so because Rider was just as much an admirer of the warden as himself and not a man to betray a confidence.

She would not have known about Gaunt's action had not a very troubled Rider come to her to talk about what he had been told. How ironic was that! His first response had been the one Gaunt had expected – one of admiration for Mr Harding's kindness – but the more he had thought about his friend's comments in regard to the danger of bringing up a murderess's child, the more his admiration had turned to anxiety. In the end it had driven him to confide in her. She had listened with mounting horror as the bedesman had begun babbling ever-increasing nonsense about how important it was that the warden should be protected – protected from the evil that would inevitably come from the daughter of the murderess. Rider had been all for telling what he knew to the bishop and the archdeacon to invoke their spiritual support. Telling him the truth – that Catherine Farrell's child was dead and that her own daughter had replaced her – was not an option she had dared risk, though with hindsight that might have been the wiser course.

Instead she had told him she knew both daughters intimately and that neither of them showed the slightest sign of inheriting the sinfulness of an evil mother. Nevertheless, it had taken all her powers of persuasion to calm his fears and keep him silent. She had recognized his silence would be temporary. And to whom else might Rider then confide the secret? He was at heart a very kind man but one who had become confused, forgetful and often muddled in his thinking. He could easily destroy the family that he so desired to assist! The idea of eliminating him had come unbidden into her head and, once implanted in her mind, it had tempted her as successfully as the serpent had tempted Eve. Rider was an old man, increasingly frail in body and mind, a man waiting for death. Why not end his needless anxieties? Why not ease his path? It had seemed so obviously the right thing to do! Why should she let an old man's pathetic and foolish fancies about inherited sin destroy her daughter's happiness?

On that fatal morning she had seen Rider go out to sit in his favourite seat and she had judged the time and place perfectly. Eleanor and Susan had just gone out for the day with Dr Grantly and Mr Harding was deeply involved in entertaining John Bold in his study. All of them would therefore have perfect alibis. As for herself, she was confident no one would ever consider her a potential murderer and, even if they did, she was sure she could get either Elias Bell or Billy Gazy to say she had been with him at the time of the murder. It was so easy to confuse them. She had wrongly thought that the police would assume some passing vagrant had committed the crime because it took place in the garden rather than the almshouse. It had seemed the perfect crime! Rider had greeted her without suspicion when she had gone out to him and she had stabbed swiftly and strongly, striking at his heart so that he would die as quickly and painlessly as possible.

But everything had gone wrong! The body had been discovered far more quickly than she had expected. Abel Handy had maliciously sought to implicate Mr Harding and his family in the murder. The inspector had not ruled out that the murder might have taken place before Dr Grantly had left with Eleanor and Susan or that Mr Harding or Mr Bold might be involved. Then there had come the sudden realization that the investigation might uncover the very secret that the murder had been committed to hide. Helpless, she had been forced to escort bedesmen into the inspector's presence, uncertain as to what they might say. And Jeremiah Smith had proved the unfortunate complication. Unbeknown to her, Thomas Rider had confided his concerns to him as well. Fortunately he had kept quiet about Mr Harding's secret adoption of Catherine Farrell's child because of his promise not to repeat what he had been told, but she knew that was but a temporary decision. And so she had been forced to kill again. Poor Smith! He had paid dearly for welcoming her into his room that evening. But so had she. His murder had removed any hope that Rider's death might be ascribed to an outsider.

She had followed the investigation with mounting alarm. Servants were invisible people, there when summoned and assumed absent when not. It had been easy for her to hear what the others were saying as she moved around the house performing her duties and, when necessary, listening at doors. Far more of the past had been uncovered than she had thought possible. The family's discovery that neither of Mr Harding's daughters was the child of Catherine Farrell did not bring her the relief it brought them. How could it? If the truth of her identity were ever discovered then her role in the murders would be immediately apparent. Her resulting arrest and trial would ruin her daughter's life and that of Mr Harding, who had so kindly brought her up. Her one crumb of comfort had been the inspector's belief that any search for Mrs Mather was unlikely to advance the investigation. He had chosen simply to send Trollope on a cursory visit to Newgate. With a bit of luck Tom Paterson would either be dead or have long since left the prison's employ.

The real threat to her was not the Post Office surveyor but John Gaunt, who might one day recognize her. And he deserved to die! It was he who had started everything by betraying the family's secret to Rider. What if she could somehow make it appear that he was the murderer? That would solve everything! All she had to do was make his death appear like a suicide and then report that he had confessed his crime to her before taking his life? But how should he die? Not by a knife blow. The answer had to be poison and she knew where to get it. In the garden there were deadly nightshade plants with their distinctive purple-brown bell-shaped flowers. She could easily pick a few and pluck up some of the plant's white, fleshy roots and extract enough poison to ensure he died speedily. All she had to do was find the best way of administering what she had prepared to him without anyone being able to point the finger of suspicion at her. Then she could be happy again!

The inspector had spent the time after Trollope had departed in another fruitless round of questioning the family and the bedesmen. On this occasion he also decided for the first time to question the housekeeper in case she might be able to provide any leads for him to follow up. Mrs Winthrop found it easy to counter his initial enquiries and to use the interview for her own ends.

'This is not the happy place Mr Harding thinks, sir,' she said in a very sad voice. 'The warden is a very kind man but, if you'll forgive me saying so, a naïve one. He does not appreciate that his kindness has led to deep divisions amongst the bedesmen.'

'What makes you say that, Mrs Winthrop?'

'When Mr Harding became warden he listened too much to those who thought his role was too well remunerated. He therefore decided to give each bedesman more money, though that was quite unnecessary because all their needs are met here.'

'But surely that would not have caused dissension?'

Mrs Winthrop shook her head, gave a sob, and, taking out her handkerchief, began wiping pretend tears from her eyes. 'It did, sir, and now I wish I'd spoken earlier. You see, I think I may know what has led to these terrible murders.'

'Come, come, Mrs Winthrop, don't upset yourself. I fail to see the connection. Explain what you mean.'

Mrs Winthrop pretended to gradually regain her composure before replying. 'Ever since the bedesmen received the extra money, they've been split into two camps. Abel Handy is the leader of one and Benjamin Bunce of the other. You've seen enough of Mr Handy to know what a malicious and greedy man he is. He's made out that the bedesmen are being robbed of what is rightfully theirs. He says that the income from Hiram's fortune should belong almost in its entirety to the bedesmen and not to the warden. He's made it appear that Mr Harding's generosity was just a sop to deceive them into an undeserved gratitude. He regularly attempts to persuade the bedesmen to sign a petition demanding they should get what is rightfully theirs.'

Blake's eyes opened wide at this new insight, which implied that the murders had nothing to do with ancient history and stemmed instead just from squabbling between the bedesmen. He looked at the agitated woman before him and sought to reassure her so that she would say more. 'Handy always was a troublemaker,' he said, nodding his head in agreement. 'I think it was an ill day Mr Harding gave him a place here.'

'I agree, sir. Happily Mr Bunce has resolutely opposed Handy's claims. Mr Bunce worships Mr Harding and will have nothing bad said of him. Thanks to his influence the petition's never got off the ground. Too many have refused to sign it.'

'I'm pleased to hear it.'

'But I think that'll now change. There's no doubt that the deaths of both Thomas Rider and Jeremiah Smith have changed the balance of power within the hospital. Mr Bunce has lost his two staunchest allies whilst Abel Handy still has the full support of Gregory Moody. They'll get both Elias Bell and Billy Gazy to do whatever they want because both men get so easily confused. It was Mr Rider and Mr Smith rather than Mr Bunce who were able to stop Handy winning over Jonathan Crumple, Job Skulpit and Matthew Spriggs. There's every chance that Mr Bunce will now face having at least seven wanting a petition. I'm not sure what the other three bedesmen will decide, but they may well, like sheep, side with the majority.' She paused for effect and then concluded, 'The more I have thought about it the more I think that it's Hiram's money that's behind the murders.'

'But Mr Handy is severely crippled. There's no way that he could have wielded the knife blows that murdered them.'

Mrs Winthrop pursed her lips. 'And that's why I've said nothing until now. But is it not possible that his insidious influence might have caused another of the bedesmen to commit the crime? It's in the nature of evil men that they often avoid the consequences of getting caught by encouraging others to do their work for them.'

The inspector jumped up, thumping the desk in front of him with his fist. 'By heaven! Mrs Winthrop, I think you've given us the clue we need to solve these murders! Although I'm tired I will at once resume questioning the bedesmen in the light of what you've told me. I just wish these old men wouldn't clam up at the mere sight of a policeman!'

'If you're prepared to delay another round of questioning, I can go around most of them tonight and try to encourage them to be more open with you tomorrow morning.'

'I would be grateful for that, Mrs Winthrop, though it might be safer for you to speak to Handy and Moody as well. Their suspicions might be aroused if they heard you were seeing everyone but them. I'll inform Mr Harding that I've given you instructions to speak with all the bedesmen this evening.'

If inwardly the housekeeper rejoiced at her success, outwardly there was no sign of this. 'Very well, sir, if that is your wish, I'll do as you say,' she answered demurely. 'I'd do anything to protect Mr Harding and his daughters.' No one listening could have doubted the honesty that lay behind that statement.

'All I ask is that you don't try to play amateur detective. I don't want the killer to strike at you because you've aroused his suspicions. If one of the bedesmen says anything that makes you think he may be responsible don't let him see that. In fact, I don't want you to say anything about what you've told me or about what any of them says to you to anyone, not even Mr Harding. You must relay anything you learn only to me. I'll expect you to report to me when I return early tomorrow morning.' He stared at her fiercely. 'I want no heroics. Leave the unmasking of the murderer to me,' he warned. 'Is that understood?'

'Rest assured, sir, I'll do exactly as you say.'

Blake smiled. 'You're a good woman, Mrs Winthrop. I'm sure that Mr Harding will reward you for your role in all this.'

'I seek no reward but to see life return to normal at the hospital, sir, and for Mr Harding and his family to be happy again,' she replied, for once speaking the truth.

No sooner had the inspector left than she began planning what to do next. There was no problem obtaining the poison but how could she persuade John Gaunt to take it? The obvious way was to put it in a drink but there was no guarantee that he would drink it. And how was she to disguise its taste? And how best should she handle seeing all the bedesmen? She knew that what she said and did in the visits to each man would be critical in getting her story accepted once Gaunt was dead. It was vital that she should play the role of a concerned friend in such a way that all the old men, if questioned, would assert how helpful she had been to each of them.

She knew the order in which she saw them also required thought because her movements were likely to be seen by one or more of them. Looking out of a window was one of the few pleasures still open to them all. As Gaunt was to die, it made sense that his home should not be the last one she was seen to visit. She should go to at least two of the bedesmen afterwards. But could she behave as if nothing had happened when she had just killed a man mere moments before? Perhaps it would help if she selected for her final visits the two who would clearly vouch for her kindness yet be least likely to note any agitation in her manner and least likely to ask her anything difficult.

The result of her deliberations was that she visited the two least important bedesmen first. The mental infirmity of Elias Bell and Billy Gazy made it quite possible that neither would even recall her visit, but she would be seen entering their homes. Next she tackled Abel Handy. The visit proved easier than she had feared because he quickly ordered her out of his room when she began talking of the importance of him co-operating more with the police. She quickly moved on to speak with first Jonathan Crumple and then Job Skulpit. Their grief at the loss of Thomas Rider and Jeremiah Smith stood out in sharp contrast to Handy's dismissive stance and she found herself genuinely offering them reassurance and comfort. Having decided to leave Matthew Spriggs and Gregory Moody till after her meeting with John Gaunt, she next saw Reuben Wilson. It was easy enough for her to twist the former miller round her finger because, despite his age, he was still a romantic and happy to flirt with her.

John Gaunt greeted her warmly when she entered his rooms and welcomed the opportunity to talk with her. 'I don't know what to do, Mrs Winthrop,' he said in a frantic tone. 'The inspector thinks I'm responsible for these murders!'

'Surely not, Mr Gaunt!'

'He does. He said that I had more or less signed poor Thomas's death warrant by informing him about Mr Harding's adoption of Catherine Farrell's child. But I meant no harm and I didn't think Thomas would tell anyone.' Tears began to fall down the former gaoler's lined cheeks. 'Ever since I confided in Mr Trollope what I knew, events seem to have passed out of my control, Mrs Winthrop, and I find that very difficult,' he bemoaned.

'I'm not surprised, Mr Gaunt. All of us like to feel we're in control of what happens around us and in your case you have also been accustomed as a former gaoler to controlling the lives of others.'

'Mr Trollope has told me that I had it all wrong anyway and that Catherine Farrell's child died years ago. There's no tainted blood flowing in the veins of either Miss Harding or Mrs Grantly.' He shook his head and Mrs Winthrop could see that he was not just distraught, he was deeply frightened that his actions would lead to him losing his place at the hospital. The shadow of the workhouse hung over him. 'So what can I do?' he muttered pathetically. 'I should never have spoken of what I knew to poor Thomas!'

'It's no good crying over spilt milk. You meant no harm. The sin lies with the person who murdered Mr Rider and Mr Smith.'

'But what must Mr Harding think of me! I promised him I would tell no one and I've brought down on his head all this sorrow!'

'Mr Harding is a very forgiving man. If you write a note saying how sorry you are for what you've done I'll take it to him.'

'I'm no writer, Mrs Winthrop. Can you help me?'

'Of course, Mr Gaunt.' She made him sit at his table, took out a piece of paper and handed him a pen. 'I would suggest the shorter the better. It will make your letter sound more from the heart.' His pen hovered over the paper but it was quickly apparent that he was struggling to know how to begin. 'Shall I help you compose what to say?' she asked. He nodded and then began to write down what she slowly dictated to him. Having signed it, he placed the letter in her hands.

'I hope this helps,' he said in a pathetic voice. 'I don't know what I'd do if Mr Harding made me leave the hospital.'

He began to weep again and she put her arm around the old man. 'Listen to me, Mr Gaunt, I'm sure Mr Harding will forgive you, especially as I'm not sure that the inspector is right about what has caused the murders. I think Mr Rider and Mr Smith died for other reasons.'

Her words instantly stopped his tears. He stared at her in surprise. 'I don't understand,' he said.

'As you well know, Abel Handy has been stirring up the bedesmen to petition the bishop about the warden's alleged abuse of Hiram's money. Both Mr Rider and Mr Smith opposed him over that matter. I think he's encouraged one of his supporters to kill them.'

Gaunt said nothing for a few moments because it took time for his ageing mind to come to terms with this latest information, but then he exclaimed, 'I think you may be right, Mrs Winthrop! Abel Handy is a malicious man and I dare say he could have encouraged his friend Moody to undertake such a deed. The two are as thick as thieves together.'

In his happiness he embraced the housekeeper. She smiled and said, 'I'm pleased you think so, Mr Gaunt, and I hope you'll sleep better tonight because of that.'

'My mind's in such a whirl that I don't think that

will be possible.'

'Now, listen to me. You look awful. You've obviously not slept since Mr Rider's death. I think the inspector would like to have your assistance tomorrow and therefore it's vitally important you sleep well tonight. Your mind will be much sharper.' She pulled out the small bottle that she had put in her apron pocket. 'Mr Bold prepared this for me because I often have a problem sleeping. You're welcome to have some.'

'That's most kind of you, Mrs Winthrop.'

'It's very effective but I warn you that it tastes rather bitter,' she replied. 'Like all good medicine the worse the taste the better it is.'

'Don't you worry. I'll drink it, whatever its taste. I want to do all I can to put Abel Handy and his accomplice behind bars and you're right in saying that a good night's sleep will make me more useful to the inspector.'

She poured the poison into a cup and handed it to him. 'I hope you have a very long sleep. Be comforted. I'm sure that by this time tomorrow the inspector will be absolutely sure who killed Mr Rider and Mr Smith.' She smiled as he took a deep gulp.

'It certainly tastes horrible!' he said. 'Can I water the rest down by adding it to my normal bedtime drink? I promise I'll take it all.'

Mrs Winthrop did not hesitate. If remnants of the poison were found in his bedtime drink it would help convince the inspector that his death was a suicide. 'Of course you can,' she said, meeting his eyes with a look of kindness.

It was only as Mrs Winthrop closed the door to Gaunt's room that she realized how much her hands were trembling. Trying to compose herself, she headed off to see the remaining two bedesmen, glad that she had chosen the two easiest for her final visits. Matthew Spriggs hardly asked her anything and spent all his time expressing his fear that he might become the next victim. Gregory Moody preferred to make the focus of their meeting how life had treated him unfairly. Having finished with him, she made her way back to the warden's house. Mr Harding made no attempt to question her. He had promised the inspector that he would not do so.

Looking at his wan and troubled face, Mrs Winthrop had not the heart to leave him entirely in the dark. 'I can't say what I've found out, sir, because I promised the inspector I would say nothing until after I've reported to him tomorrow. However, I want you to know that I've obtained enough information to know who the murderer is. Moreover, I think he'll confess to the inspector tomorrow morning. He's also given me a letter to give to you. Rest assured, sir. All the members of your family are innocent. So too is Mr Bold.'

Mr Harding could hardly believe what she had told him. 'Bless you, bless you, Mrs Winthrop. You don't know what this means to me! I feel as if I've been released from the depths of hell.' He turned away so as to hide his emotion. Despite all his love, he had begun to wonder whether Eleanor or Susan or John Bold had committed the murders and he had hated himself for doing so. His housekeeper's words restored a peace that he thought he had lost forever.

'No, don't you go fretting yourself any more, sir. We'll all be happy again.'

He turned to face her but his joy was marred by the sadness her words evoked. 'I don't think, Mrs Winthrop, this place will ever be the same happy place to me again. I'm not sure I was the right choice to be made warden if such horrors as we've seen can occur under my watch.'

'Nonsense, sir. No man is more suited to being the warden of Hiram's Hospital.'

'You're most kind.'

'I say no more than you deserve, sir, and I hope that I can serve you and your family until the day I die.'

Mr Harding was visibly touched by her loyalty. 'If your work this evening has brought our suffering to an end by tomorrow, then you will have earned far more than that right. You will have our undying gratitude.'

Mrs Winthrop fought back her tears.

12

THE TRAGIC OUTCOME

THE NEXT MORNING Mrs Winthrop reported to the inspector that her discussions with the bedesmen had confirmed that the murders stemmed from greedy squabbling. He totally accepted her version of her meetings and so hardly asked any questions. He was only taken aback when she said that the murderer was John Gaunt.

'What makes you say that? I would've thought him one of the least likely candidates,' he said, rubbing his chin with left hand.

'I admit I wouldn't have chosen him as the guilty person until I saw how much he was wracked with guilt. Believe me, sir, I obeyed your instructions and I did not try to interrogate him, but he more or less confessed to me. I've something here that he asked me to give to Mr Harding.' She took out a small envelope from her apron pocket.

'Then why have you not done so?'

'Mr Gaunt made me promise I would delay handing its contents over until today. I thought I ought to report the matter to you before giving it to Mr Harding this morning.'

'I see.' He reached out his hand. 'Give the letter to me.'

Mrs Winthrop instinctively drew away and plunged the envelope back into her apron. 'I'm sorry, sir, but I can't do that. I gave my word that I would hand it over only to Mr Harding.'

The inspector hid his annoyance and opened the study door. He bellowed for Mr Harding and Dr Grantly to come and join them. The warden and archdeacon at once came from the parlour, where they had been anxiously awaiting the outcome of Mrs Winthrop's report.

'Mrs Winthrop has a letter addressed to you, Mr Harding, from John Gaunt. It may contain a confession. She won't give it to me so please tell her to give it to you. Then open it, and read what it says,' he commanded. 'I want to know what it contains before I see him.'

White faced, Mr Harding took the envelope containing the letter from his housekeeper. His hands trembled as he opened it. Then he read out in a shaky voice:

Dear Mr Harding,

I'm sorry for all that I have done. I know that I've let you down and that you and your family have suffered as a result. That was not my intention. I don't know what led me to do it. It was a moment of sinful weakness. And now Thomas and Jeremiah are dead because of me. Please find it in your heart to forgive me. My life seems worthless now. John Gaunt

Dr Grantly grabbed the letter from the warden and quietly re-read it. He smiled. 'It would seem we have our murderer, Inspector.'

'I cannot believe it, not John,' Mr Harding muttered. 'What possible motive could he have?'

'There's been more dissension between the bedesmen than you know, Mr Harding,' commented Mrs Winthrop. 'In a small place like this disagreements can seem far more important than they are.'

'Dr Grantly and Mrs Winthrop, will you go and fetch Mr Gaunt?' asked the inspector. 'We can then hear direct what led him to do these terrible crimes.'

The archdeacon and housekeeper nodded and left the study to set out for the almshouse. No sooner had they left the warden's house than they were aware something must have happened because virtually all the bedesmen were gathered around a wailing man. As they drew nearer they saw this was Jonathan Crumple and heard the cause – he had discovered the dead body of John Gaunt. Dr Grantly was genuinely shocked and no observer could have imagined anything other than that Mrs Winthrop was equally taken by surprise. Suppressing his emotion, the archdeacon quickly took command of the situation, shouting at Crumple, 'Take control of yourself, man, and take me to Mr Gaunt's room so I can examine the body for myself.'

It was not long before they re-emerged. Crumple immediately began walking to the warden's house, while the archdeacon looked around him at the fearful faces of the eight remaining bedesmen. He said quietly, 'By the look of Mr Gaunt he's been poisoned, but I want no panic here. I think he died by his own hand. I've sent Mr Crumple to collect the inspector.'

The confirmation of Gaunt's death and the statement that it was probably suicide led to considerable murmuring between the old men, and none noted the response of Mrs Winthrop until she fell to the ground as if she had fainted. Dr Grantly immediately moved to assist her. 'Mr Bunce, help me with Mrs Winthrop,' he shouted. 'Let's see if we can get her sat down on that garden seat. The shock has been too much for the poor woman. The rest of you get indoors now!'

The bedesmen were too stunned by a third death to do anything but obey, even the normally obstructive Handy. All but Benjamin Bunce had returned to their rooms by the time the inspector and the warden came running to the scene. 'Mr Gaunt is definitely dead and I'm pretty sure that he's taken poison,' Dr Grantly said bluntly as they drew up to where he and Bunce were reviving the housekeeper. 'It looks to me as if our murderer has meted out his own justice!'

'What do you mean by that?' asked a puzzled Bunce.

'John Gaunt has left a note for Mr Harding confessing that he killed Thomas Rider and Jeremiah Smith,' replied Dr Grantly curtly.

Bunce's face filled with horror. 'I don't believe it. He was a good man, a man of faith. He would not have done such a thing.'

The warden shook his head sadly. 'There's no doubt about the matter, my friend. I've a letter in his own handwriting.'

'Then I have lost all faith in my ability to judge the

worth of a man,' mumbled Bunce and he appeared to visibly age before their eyes.

Dr Grantly looked at the housekeeper, who still appeared dazed. 'Mr Harding, I suggest you escort Mrs Winthrop back to your house with Mr Bunce's assistance. She has had a terrible shock. Tell Susan and Eleanor what has happened and get them to tend to her.'

'And then send someone for Mr Bold,' added the inspector. 'Dr Grantly, I suggest that you check all the bedesmen are back inside their rooms. Tell them that there will not be any more murders and that they are all safe now. I want them all to stay indoors until the doctor has been and an undertaker has removed John Gaunt's body for further investigation. While you're doing that I'll take a look at the body.'

The inspector entered the almshouse and went to the old man's room. Gaunt's contorted body was lying on the bed. There was a strange red rash across his face, which was set in a rictus grin of startled alarm. Blake looked around and immediately spotted there was an empty cup on the man's table. The inspector raised it to his nose and sniffed. What had he taken?

While these events were taking place, Anthony Trollope was already on the train from Waterloo. The line to Salisbury, which had only opened in 1847, had reduced the time required to get between the two cities to less than three hours. Nevertheless, it was not until well after midday that he arrived back at Hiram's Hospital. Immediately he sensed something was wrong. There was not a bedesman in sight. Running up to the warden's house, he thundered for admittance. It was Mrs Winthrop who opened the door. He stared at her, desperately trying to judge whether he could be right in his surmise that this woman was Mrs Mather. She had all the appearance of respectability. Surely he must be wrong? She did not look like a murderess. But could such a distinctive scar be a coincidence?

'We didn't expect you back so soon, Mr Trollope,' she said, stepping aside to let him in. 'Have your enquiries in London led to any useful information?'

'That remains to be seen, Mrs Winthrop,' he replied ambivalently, averting his eyes lest she saw his newfound suspicion of her.

'You may have had a wasted journey, sir, because you'll be pleased to hear that the murderer is uncovered. He has confessed and the family is all cleared of any involvement.'

Trollope's mind reeled. Then his conjecture about the housekeeper must be wrong! 'Who was it?' he gasped.

'John Gaunt. He left a note before committing suicide.'

'I can't believe it! I talked often with the man.'

'It's come as a great shock to us all, sir.'

'Where's Mr Harding?'

'Everyone is in the parlour with the inspector.'

'Please show me in to them at once.'

The housekeeper courteously inclined her head and did as she was bid. It was only after he had entered the room and she stood alone in the corridor that she permitted her true feelings to show in her face. Her earlier euphoria at her plan's success had all gone. Trollope was no actor and she knew beyond question that he now distrusted her because of what he had uncovered in London. He had not looked her fully in the face. Mrs Winthrop bit her lip and sought to control the mounting tide of despair that was sweeping over her. All her senses told her that he must have discovered her real identity, and if that were the case she had no doubt that the inspector would reopen his investigation. If that happened, Gaunt's letter and subsequent death would not be accepted at their face value. What should she do? Had she time to make her escape? And if so, where could she go?

Inside the parlour Trollope's arrival, combined with his agitated manner, was causing equal consternation.

'Why have you returned so soon?' Blake asked.

'Is it true that John Gaunt is dead?' Trollope responded tremulously.

'I'm afraid so,' said Mr Harding. 'John has just been telling us the results of his medical examination of the body. He suspects Gaunt poisoned himself with belladonna.'

'What's that?'

'A poison derived from deadly nightshade,' answered Bold. 'There's a huge patch of it growing in the garden. The poor man would not have suffered much at first. The drug's initial action would have been only to impair his eyesight and give him a thirst. That's because it dilates the eyes and suppresses the saliva in your mouth. As it took hold he would have felt his pulse beginning to race and seen that he was developing a rash across his neck and body. However,

I don't envy him his last hours. He would have had terrible hallucinations until he fell into a stupor. Death results from respiratory paralysis.'

'It appears he could no longer live with his crimes,' interrupted the inspector and he proceeded to briefly outline all that happened since Trollope's departure the previous afternoon.

'May I see the letter that he wrote?'

Blake took it out of his pocket and, as he passed it to Trollope, stated, 'You'll see it's pretty conclusive.'

Trollope read its contents as the others looked on in silence. 'I agree it would appear so,' he said once he had finished. Then, biting his lip with frustration, he continued, 'But I fear we can't take this at face value because of the reason that has brought me back here so quickly.'

'I don't understand. What evidence could possibly be stronger than a suicide note?' said Dr Grantly.

Trollope chose to counter this with his own question. 'Is there any person here who would have expected John Gaunt to be capable of such crimes?'

'I certainly find it very hard to think him of him as a murderer,' replied the warden.

'And I,' said John Bold.

'That's just your inexperience showing,' grumbled the inspector. 'I've dealt with enough crimes to know that in certain circumstances men can behave totally out of character.'

'Yes, if their mind is affected, but I'll vouch for the fact that John Gaunt's mind was as sharp as ever. He was genuinely fearful that he might become the next victim. All my dealings with him convince me he's innocent. I think this letter must be open to another explanation.'

'How can that be?' uttered Mrs Grantly. 'I hope, sir, that you're not going to plunge this family into further agonies by giving out that the letter is a forgery.'

'No, it's no forgery but under what circumstances was it written? How did it come into your possession?'

'Mrs Winthrop brought it,' Blake replied. 'She visited all the bedesmen last night and Gaunt more or less admitted his guilt to her and gave her the letter to give to Mr Harding this morning.'

'And would it affect your judgement if I told you that I'm almost certain that Mrs Winthrop is Mrs Mather?' There was a deep intake of breath from his audience. 'That's what my visit to Newgate uncovered. That's why I have returned so quickly.' Before any of them could speak he began recounting all that Tom Paterson had told him and what conclusion he had drawn from it.

'Are you daring to say that either I or my sister has our housekeeper as our mother?' raged Mrs Grantly once he had finished. 'How dare you! You've not a shred of evidence. This is mere supposition. There are plenty of women in this world with scars on their faces. I'd rather put my faith in the letter. That's what I call evidence!'

'Let me see it again,' said Blake, reaching out his hand. He slowly re-read the note and then thrust it into the warden's hand. 'I think we've been naïve, Mr Harding. Look again at it. All this letter says is that Gaunt wants your forgiveness for letting you down and telling your secret. It does not say that he killed

Rider and Smith. It simply says that they would still be alive if he'd kept his mouth shut.'

'No! I refuse to believe it!' Mrs Grantly stormed. 'Summon Mrs Winthrop! I'm sure that she'll be able to prove that she's not Mrs Mather. She'll put pay to such nonsense. Gaunt more or less confessed to her!'

'So she said, but I'm not so sure,' ventured Eleanor. 'I'm sorry to say it, sister, but I think Mr Trollope and the inspector are likely to be right and that poor Mr Gaunt was simply her third victim. Think back, Susan. For years we've been shown nothing but love by Mrs Winthrop. Far more love than we sometimes deserved. Perhaps it was a mother's love that we experienced, not that of a mere housekeeper. She loved one of us – the one who is her daughter – enough to kill three men rather than let their loose tongues envelop this family in scandal.'

Her words moved all the men but not Mrs Grantly, who glowered angrily at them all. 'For months I thought I might be the child of a murderer and I feared that information might destroy our family. Have you any idea how much I've suffered? There's not been a day when I've not looked at my husband and wondered whether the news of my ancestry would somehow come to light and destroy his reputation and his career. There's not been a day when I've not looked at our children and feared what mockery they would face from others. And yet you ask me now to believe that I might be the child of a woman who has killed not once but thrice! You ask me to accept what I know would tarnish the name of Harding and Grantly beyond any redemption. No, I'll not believe it!'

'I suggest, Mr Trollope, that you and Mr Bold go fetch Mrs Winthrop,' ordered Blake, breaking the uneasy silence that followed Mrs Grantly's impassioned speech. 'I suggest that the rest of us say no more until I've questioned her. The one thing I guarantee is that no one will be leaving this room until these crimes are finally solved!'

For the next few minutes each person pursued his or her own thoughts and the only movement in the room was provided by Mr Harding's silent playing of his imaginary violincello. Such was their own agonized suspense that for once neither of the warden's daughters moved to comfort their father in his distress. All eyes were focused entirely on the door. However, when it opened, only Trollope entered. His face was ashen white and in his hand he clutched a red-stained note. He stared at their anxious faces and then grimly announced, 'I regret to say that Mrs Winthrop has slit her wrists. We found her dead body in her room. Mr Bold is attending to matters.' He paused and his lips trembled. 'I suggest that none of you go there yet. There's blood everywhere.' Mr Harding ceased his playing as his daughter Eleanor flung herself into his arms in her horror at the news. 'She left this note,' Trollope concluded, looking at Mrs Grantly. 'It's addressed to you.'

Mrs Grantly, overcome with emotion, burst into tears, and her husband quickly moved to comfort her. Blake reached out and took the note from Trollope's hand. He quickly read its contents and then looked at the others. 'It's signed Elizabeth Mather and, with Mrs Grantly's permission, I think you should all hear this,' he said quietly.

'I care not who hears what she has to say. She's destroyed us all!' she groaned in reply.

Blake read the letter again but this time out loud:

Dearest daughter – for that is what you are – please forgive me. I have experienced such joy in watching you grow up surrounded by nothing but love and kindness. No mother could be prouder than I am of what you have become – a dutiful daughter, a loving sister, a worthy wife, a kind mother. I never intended to harm so many innocent people but I loved you too much and one sin led to another. I say that not as an excuse for my actions but as an explanation. Nothing can excuse what I have done. I know that now.

God knows I have suffered enough in my life but I've also witnessed great kindness, especially in this house. I could not have wished for a better master than the man who became your loving father. I have repaid his kindness ill and I welcome an end to all my deceit. I saw from Mr Trollope's face that he knew my true identity when he arrived today. I end my life so that you and Eleanor and Mr Harding are spared the horror of a trial with all the adverse publicity that would attend that.

Please tell your father – for he has earned that title by action if not through blood – that I truly repent of what I've done these past few days but not of entrusting my child to his care. I can't repent doing that, even if it means I have to face all the torments of hell. I hope he will find it in his heart to pray for me. Please tell Eleanor that I loved her as much as I loved you. I hope that she will find as good a husband as you have found. She deserves no less.

I pray that Mr Blake will have the kindness not to tell the world what led to my actions. He can say that poor Mrs Winthrop was struck down by a madness – a madness that led her first to kill others and then herself. Then no one need know that you are my child and there will be no scandal. There will simply be a momentary stir and all will be soon forgotten.

Please forgive me, and, if you can't do that, please forget me. Live as if I had never been. I don't know whether a woman who has sinned as much as I have can offer a blessing to anyone, but, if God is willing, let my blessing fall on you and those you love.

Blake handed the letter to Dr Grantly. 'I suggest, sir, that you destroy this. Let there be no evidence of the link between your wife and the dead woman. As far as I'm concerned this case is closed. Mr Bold can certify that Mrs Winthrop was not in her right mind and I'll report to the outside world that a woman's insanity was responsible for three murders. Madness requires no motive for what has taken place here.' He turned to Trollope and added, 'Do you agree with my conclusions on this case, sir?'

Trollope smiled. 'You've expressed my feelings on the matter with admirable precision, Mr Blake.'

Nothing was said by Mr Harding or his daughters but their faces bespoke their gratitude.

AFTERWORD

THE WRITING OF *THE WARDEN*

THE RELEASE OF Inspector Blake's information on the three murders at Hiram's Hospital kept tongues busy in Barchester for a number of days. Many reasons were invented as to what might have driven the housekeeper insane. None came remotely near the truth. Her prediction proved correct. It was not long before the story soon ceased to be news. People's minds turned to other issues that were taking place in the city and in the country.

The lives of all those connected with Hiram's Hospital appeared to return to normal. Mr Harding resumed his duties as warden and was pleased to receive into his care three new bedesmen to replace those who had died. Miss Harding and Mr Bold continued to see each other although Dr Grantly and his wife remained opposed to the young doctor as a prospective suitor. All of them avoided speaking of their former housekeeper but that did not mean that she was forgotten. How could she be? Her love – and the actions that had stemmed from it – had touched them all forever.

Unfortunately scandal of another form was soon to affect Mr Harding. The issue of the use of John Hiram's money resurfaced because the deaths of Thomas Rider, Jeremiah Smith and John Gaunt paved the way for Abel Handy to achieve a victory over Benjamin Bunce. The former stonemason persuaded the majority of the new body of bedesmen into signing a petition against the Church's wrongful use of the money from Hiram's legacy. Anyone wanting to know more about what happened can read Anthony Trollope's novel, *The Warden*, which was published in 1856. However, they will find there are no references in that book to the existence of Catherine Farrell or Mrs Winthrop. Trollope had no need to disclose the secret that had so nearly destroyed the lives of Mr Harding and his daughters. Indeed, he took the precaution of altering the age of Mrs Grantly in his novel and making it appear as if she were much older than Eleanor and the real mother of her husband's children. In that way he knew none could possibly link her with either of the dead women.

The Warden achieved the success that Trollope's earlier books had been denied. As a consequence he ceased his work for the Post Office and become one of the most popular novelists of the late nineteenth century. Five of his later novels contained further stories about events in and around Barchester, or, as it is more commonly known, Salisbury.